Lady C. Investigates

Book Three

Issy Brooke

CHAPTER ONE

Southern England, Spring 1846

"But Mrs Jepson is a narrow-minded, pinched-up, grey-hearted fossil and I don't care one whit for anything she might say." Cordelia, Lady Cornbrook slammed shut the lid of the hefty trunk and stood back, folding her arms defiantly.

Her maid, the buxom and somewhat boisterous Ruby, rolled her eyes as she turned away, and Cordelia caught the rude gesture. "My lady," Ruby replied, almost politely, at least by Ruby's standards. "If I might be so bold. She did have a point about the way you focused *quite* so much on yeast in that last article you wrote. Remember that your audience is a well-bred and refined one, who do not want to think in depth about ... about how they are consuming fungus."

"Well-bred," Cordelia said, struck by a sudden notion. "Bred. *Bread!* Aha. I must make that pun in a future column."

Ruby shrugged and sighed, and said blandly, "Indeed, my lady. I am sure that your readers will be howling in their drawing rooms."

"You do mean howling with laughter, don't you?"

"I must go to the kitchens and ensure the food is being packed for the journey."

Ruby sashayed out of the dressing room, leaving Cordelia alone with her thoughts.

But they were not maudlin thoughts. How could they be? Here she was, an independent lady of means, in her own house, and truly mistress of her own destiny.

Furthermore, it was the very cusp of spring and the grounds of her house were filled with great swathes of daffodils and crocuses, in a display that one visitor had called "positively indecent". Such an accolade had filled Cordelia with delight.

She still received visitors, and she was grateful for that. She was, at least in principle, a respectable widow. Her titled husband had died and after some wrangling she had won the right to live in their marital home, Clarfields.

But in many other respects, she was simply *not quite right*. She had not remarried, in spite of offers, but nor did she withdraw herself into a quiet seclusion. Instead she had thrust herself out into the world as a *sole femme* and in doing so, ruffled some well-to-do feathers.

Cordelia left the dressing room and went to her study. It was a pleasant room on the west side of the house, and she found she did her best thinking as the evening rays of the sun filled the place with warm light. Now, in the early morning, it was cool and dark. She wanted to pack her notebooks and letter-writing supplies, and of course, some copies of her recently-published column.

She couldn't help smiling as she picked up the latest edition of the weekly household magazine that she was now writing for. This was her third column to appear in print, and she was pleased that it seemed to be well-received — well, if one ignored Mrs Jepson. And that harridan who had spoken so harshly at last week's soiree. Oh, and the nasty anonymous letter that appeared in a local parish magazine.

And a few other dissenters, too, who could be also be disregarded.

Yes, apart from all those ignorant people, it was a well-received column indeed.

She folded the magazine and placed it in a board-backed portfolio case with the other copies. She realised that she kept pausing to think, and that her thoughts were skittering around, easily distracted by new and almost unrelated thoughts, like a squirrel let loose in a nut store.

But it was spring, and she was happy, and she was going to visit London. So, why not! She could allow herself a moment to relax and daydream. Her new life was beginning, at last.

***

"Mrs Unsworth threw a sausage at me," Ruby said unhappily when they met again in Cordelia's dressing room, later.

"Why? What did you say to her?"

"Absolutely nothing! So then she accused me of ignoring her. Must we take her to London with us, my lady?"

"We must. It is essential that we have a cook with us."

"No one cooks in London. Not at home, at any rate. Why would they?"

"Well, we shall. I have taken rooms that have a small kitchen attached. I do not know how Gibbs managed it, but he is a miracle worker. It is imperative that I am able to continue my research into the regional foods of Britain. My column — my fans! — demand it. I am particularly interested in whelks."

"No one is interested in whelks."

"Then I shall stir up that interest. Oh, Ruby, I am so excited! I feel as if I am on the very edge of things, new things, amazing things. It is almost tangible." She wanted to dance around the room, but her maid's pained expression prevented her.

It wasn't just the new career or the forthcoming trip.

8

Indeed, Cordelia could feel a general optimism within society itself. Their beautiful young monarch, Queen Victoria, was expecting her fifth child and the vibrant, growing Royal household was the toast of the Empire. Even her dashing husband of six years, Albert, was growing in popularity as he took more of a role in charitable endeavours, and they had sparked quite a debate in many circles. The world was shiny and new and full of promise.

Ruby flipped open the trunk that Cordelia had previously slammed shut. "All these gowns are light and thin," she remarked. "You need to dress for any weather. If I may suggest, my lady, perhaps—"

There was a faint tapping at the door. Ruby and Cordelia looked at one another in surprise. The knock was tentative and barely audible.

"Only Stanley would knock like that," Ruby said. "But that boy would rather eat a shoe than come up here to your personal quarters."

That same sentiment was true of most of her staff. Ruby, as lady's maid, had privileges not extended to the rest of the household. There were maids in the lower rooms that Cordelia had never even seen.

There was a pause, then the knocking resumed, but a little louder this time.

"Go and see," Cordelia ordered.

Ruby smoothed down her skirts — after all, it might be anyone out there in the corridor, and it didn't do to be unprepared — and opened the door with a flourish.

She let her hand drop and her shoulders relax. "Oh," she said. "It's only Mr Fry, the butler. Get up, Mr Fry. Why are you crying?"

CHAPTER TWO

It took them fifteen minutes to entice the gibbering, prostrate Neville Fry into a semi-public receiving room on the ground floor of Clarfields. He would not enter her dressing room, of course, and nor would she invite him there. But he refused to come into her study and barely made sense when she tried to talk to him in the corridor.

Now he was perched on the very edge of a chair in the large blue-themed receiving room, clutching a glass of brandy. He was not so much thin, as he was narrow, as if he had been a standard sort of man until he had been pressed firmly between two planks, making him become tall and straight-edged.

And "straight-edged" usually described the man's normal nature, too. He took to the art of butlering with the precision of a military commander planning a large campaign. The staff beneath him did not always enjoy his rigid rule, but at least everyone knew exactly what was expected of them, even if they could barely ever hope to meet those expectations.

And they had also learned to keep a measuring tape handy. Neville Fry liked accuracy in all things.

That accuracy was not currently extended to his communication skills. He sipped at the fiery alcohol, and tried to make his words come in order.

"They've arrested my daughter, my lady!"

He then burbled a little about politics, for some reason, and Cordelia cut him short. "Hold on, Mr Fry. Let us return to the first thing. Your ... *daughter?*"

Ruby was keeping a polite distance, standing at the window and looking out over the floral-edged lawns. She did not turn to face them, but Cordelia knew that she would be feeling the same shock that Cordelia did.

As far as everyone had been aware, Neville Fry was not married. It wasn't really encouraged. If your butler had a wife, his loyalties would be divided.

He was red in the face, from brandy and passion and shame. "My daughter, Florence," he mumbled to the thin carpet at his feet.

"And how old is Florence? And her mother?" Cordelia probed, kicking her way through the norms of polite conversation. This was too important to be tactful about.

"Florence is, um, around twenty-two, now, I believe, my lady. And, er, her mother ... suffice it to say that we are no longer together. But we were married. No, we are still married, of course," he added hastily.

"You've been in service at Clarfields for longer than I have been here," she pointed out. "Unless you've been keeping your wife hidden in a cellar — and I do hope not, for she could have been working for me and being useful instead — then of course you are no longer together." *Well, well,* she thought, a hint of admiration clouding her mind. *Laced-up Neville Fry was once unlaced.* "Have you any other offspring, living or dead?"

"No, my lady," he said, and shuddered.

Once was clearly enough for him, she thought. "And so you have no contact with your family?"

"It was best, for all concerned, if I absented myself and left them to make their own way," he said. "And they refused my money," he added, his voice growing clearer for a moment before he remembered his current situation and stifled another sob. "But they need my help now!"

"And what of this politician you mentioned?" she said.

Neville threw back the remains of the brandy and placed the glass with a heavy click onto a side table before burying his face in his knobbly hands. "They say she has killed him!"

"Ooh!" Cordelia exclaimed with such glee that Ruby spun around and shot her mistress a warning stare. Cordelia managed to modify her exclamation into a drawn-out "ohhhh ... how ... awful."

Bit by bit, the rest of the story emerged. She whetted him with a little more brandy until she had learned that Florence was being held in the cells of a police station in London, awaiting trial for the murder of a prominent politician called Bonneville. Neville could not explain why or how his daughter had been arrested for the crime. He could not even say at what trade the girl worked, or if she were married, or anything useful.

Cordelia's mind leaped to the first and most unsavoury conclusion, but she did not want to express that to the distraught father. Instead, she turned to Ruby, and tried to sound solemn and respectful as she said, "We shall leave directly after luncheon. Will you see to the necessary arrangements with all haste, Ruby? We are nearly ready to depart, after all."

"The carriage? Won't Geoffrey need time to—"

"He can get the travelling chariot ready in an instant, I am sure. He knew we were to go to London within the next few days. Go and unearth Stanley, and Mr Fry, you need to be ready to leave also."

"Why the haste?" Ruby muttered as she moved to the

door, but did not go through it.

"We have a murder!" Cordelia trilled, almost clapping her hands. She fought down her glee and reminded herself that someone was dead. And here was a man for whom she was responsible, and he needed her help.

Neville got up, but stumbled and collapsed to his knees. Cordelia placed her hand on his shoulder, and he looked almost about to throw his arms around her skirts in a dramatic gesture. She shuffled back slightly, removing her hand.

"Thank you, my lady!" he said. "I am sure that one word from you in the ears of the police there, and they will realise it has all been a dreadful misunderstanding, and release her immediately!"

"Of course, of course," she said. "Now, I feel that it is best for you that you are busy. Go and see to the table, and make it ready for lunch." He would be better if he were occupied, she knew.

Neville struggled to his feet and took his leave. Ruby opened the door for him and watched him go.

"Go on," Cordelia said. "To Geoffrey, and to Stanley."

Ruby half-smiled. "So you are to put word in the ear of the police?" she said. "That is your aim, is it not?"

Cordelia gave her a broad grin in return.

"And there is a murder to solve!"

CHAPTER THREE

They packed awkwardly into the travelling chariot that would take them to the railway station. Clarfields was not far from London but Cordelia would not use the large, heavy coach in the capital city's narrow and crowded streets. Geoffrey, her solid and intimidating coachman, sat up top on the high front seat with the boy, Stanley. Within the plush purple interior, Mrs Unsworth ensconced her plump and unformed frame deep in a corner and half-closed her eyes, refusing to interact in any way. She was an excellent cook but a foul character and no one missed her lack of conversation. Cordelia imagined that the staff remained behind at Clarfields would currently be celebrating their freedom from the professed cook's tyranny.

Ruby and Cordelia sat side by side, and Neville completed the quartet inside the coach. He was excruciatingly embarrassed at the close proximity to

Cordelia, and desperately folded in on himself. He was the highest-ranking servant at Clarfields, and lorded it over the rest of the household, but when he was in Cordelia's presence he could barely function unless by the set and recommended ways. If it wasn't proscribed in a manual, he could not do it.

"Have you packed clothing such as might be appropriate to solving a murder, Ruby?" Cordelia asked.

"What, like a large and menacing cloak?"

"Just so," Cordelia said, wondering if Ruby were jesting or not. "I don't think I have one suitable. I must acquire one."

"Solving a murder, my lady?" Neville spoke in a hushed tone as the chariot lurched and rocked, and then began its slow progress to the station. He would not have usually spoken out of turn, but his whole world had been shaken out of alignment.

"Oh, well, only as a natural by-product of getting your poor daughter freed," she assured him hastily, raising her voice above the clatter and racket of the carriage wheels. "It simply occurs to me that effecting her release from custody might be more easily done if I am able to offer up the real culprit. After all, did you say it was a politician who has died? They must have a queue of people wishing to do them harm, I would imagine. I can no longer read the

18

papers at breakfast, for fear of running amok with a knife when I learn of the latest idiocies being committed by so-called learned men in Parliament."

Neville dug into his jacket pocket. Due to his worry and distraction, he had not changed for the journey, and was still dressed in his typical butler's daytime attire of neat pepper-and-salt trousers, black dress coat and high-cut waistcoat. In contrast to Geoffrey the coachman, Neville was generally meticulous in his dress. He had the neatest fingernails that Cordelia had ever seen and she often wondered what his secret was. It was the mark of a very good butler; they said that only a lowly waiter would wear gloves when serving, because that showed he needed to hide his work-roughened hands. She watched them as he pulled out a folded letter and passed it to Cordelia. "From Florence," he said.

The handwriting was very small, and some words were partly written in a shaky copperplate and others were partly in capital letters. It was from the hand of someone who had learned to write in their childhood, but who had had precious little practise or opportunity since then.

"My dearest father," it began, and that raised Cordelia's eyebrows. *Really?* "I am sorry to be writing to you in such terrible circumstances." The original was spelled incorrectly, Cordelia noted, and she fought the urge to pull out a pen and mark it up. She certainly ensured that she *read* it with the correct spellings sounding out in her head. "I have been taken under arrest in the most foul of ways and they do hold me here in the police station house at Bow Street and indeed I do not know what they intend to do with me save for they are loud and brutish men here and the prisoners are nearly as bad." *Who are loud and brutish if not the prisoners? Oh, the policemen themselves,* she realised. Peel's new police. Or, as the papers would have it, New Police. For they were Very Important Men.

The letter continued in its rambling way. "They are saying most wrongly that I did kill Louis, that is Mr Bonneville, but I could never lay a hand unto such a man."

Why not, Cordelia thought. *Is — was — he too strong, or was he your master, or was this as sordid as I suspect it might have been? But you would not call your master by his first name. So...*

The letter concluded with many entreaties for help and assured Neville of her undying love and devotion as a daughter.

"May I keep this?" she asked Neville and he nodded.

"My lady, what think you to this?"

"I think it exceedingly strange," she said, and tucked the letter into her tasselled green bag.

***

At the railway station, they went their separate ways. Stanley and Geoffrey took the trunks and boxes to the goods van. Cordelia called Stanley back briefly before he headed to the second class coaches.

"Will you buy me the latest London papers?" she asked, passing him some money. "Anything that mentions this politician, Louis Bonneville, or the murder."

He scampered off.

Mrs Unsworth was clutching her own personal travelling bag, a large and sagging affair made of thick fabric with wooden handles. She hovered by Cordelia and Ruby until she, too, was sent to the second class carriages, Neville Fry trailing behind. Although third class carriages were now enclosed from the weather, she had decided to pay for her staff to travel with a little more comfort.

Even so, Mrs Unsworth scowled at Ruby before lumbering away.

"She does not take well to me being favoured so highly," Ruby said as she followed Cordelia to their first class coach. "She thinks that she ranks above me."

"In some ways, she does. But I could hardly travel alone," Cordelia said. They reached an open door and the guard helped them both into a small, boxy space. "I have read all manner of dreadful insults being perpetrated on women who are stuck, quite alone and helpless. As the train rushes on, through the horrible darkness of tunnels, all kinds of crimes can be committed." She shuddered. "Keep your wits about you. Trust no one, watch everyone, and be ready to strike out at the first hint of trouble."

Ruby smiled. "I should think the other passengers have more to fear from us, in truth."

There was only one other in the coach, and they looked up in alarm as they could not help overhearing Ruby's words. Cordelia and Ruby took two of the three seats along one wall, with their backs to the engine. The afore-mentioned other occupant, a man in the garb of a well-heeled and well-fed country landowner, tipped his hat and returned his attention to the small book in his hands.

The other three seats were unoccupied and Cordelia stretched out her legs in an unwomanly way. The upholstery was thin and the horsehair fabric felt rough even through the thin cotton of her gloves, but at least there was padding on these seats.

The rest of her staff would be on wooden benches.

She unfolded the first newspaper with a snap as the guard slammed the door and trapped them within. There was no way, now, of communicating with any other carriage or compartment, and if one needed help, the only solution was to poke one's head from the window and hope that the guard was looking forwards from his own window.

"Now," she said, half to Ruby and half to herself. "Let us discover what this Bonneville is about."

The train eased forward, jerked, stuttered, and began to pick up speed by slow and steady degrees. The whistle blew a few times. The sound always thrilled Cordelia. It spoke of modernity and glory and the potential to be *somewhere else*. And quickly, too.

She had to hunt through long thin columns of advertisements until she alighted upon a story reporting the murder but it told her precious little beyond the fact that "the killer was already in custody after being apprehended at the scene" and "the well-known politician would be a sad loss to the House."

There was also an opinion piece from a minister of religion who used it as a jumping-off point for his advice about women covering their heads in church.

She read the paper again, front to back, but there was nothing to tell her about Bonneville. At the next station, the landowner alighted, and she cursed her reticence; she could have, perhaps, pumped him for information.

"These new police," she mused as she folded the paper back up. "The darlings of the right honourable Sir Robert Peel himself. I do not think I have seen them. I was a girl in London, and it was many years ago."

Ruby made a disparaging sound. "The crushers," she

said. "I think they only want change for change's sake but they are no better than the watch and the runners before them."

"Oh really? And is that your own studied and educated opinion, Ruby, or are you merely parroting to me something that you have heard others say?"

"Well, my lady, it's true that it's only what I've heard." Ruby had a mulish look on her pretty face. "But that is important, even so. To know what others think, that's as useful as knowing the truth, to my mind."

"Hmm, I hate to admit you might have a point. So I shan't. But thank you for your input," Cordelia said. She looked down at the paper and knew that Ruby was pulling a triumphant face at her; she selectively ignored the insurrection. *Let her win the little battles,* she thought. *I will always win the war.* And she liked Ruby's forthrightness.

Her words were interesting. *Yes,* Cordelia thought. *Knowing what others think is as useful as knowing the truth itself. What has more weight? Public opinion, of course, and facts be damned!*

Which boded ill for a poor girl arrested for murder.

She straightened up, and said to Ruby, "We need to know *some* facts, however. We need to discover who the enemies of this Bonneville were. And we need to find out if this poor Florence was targeted deliberately and used for someone's nefarious purpose, or whether she was

24

meaningless, and simply in the way."

Ruby nodded. Both women fell into thought as the steam locomotive dragged them through the green fields and now into London itself.

Outside, the air changed from clear to a faded, scruffy yellow, and the sky seemed to lower upon the black buildings and twisted narrow streets.

"What a pit of filth," Cordelia murmured.

"You're smiling again," remarked Ruby.

CHAPTER FOUR

London! How it had changed since Cordelia's girlhood. Twenty years ago, even ten years past, and it had been so very different. The railway had not come, then, and when she had been there, she had stuck to only frequenting a certain narrow and respectable area, and even then she had always been accompanied or chaperoned.

When she had travelled from place to place in the great city, she had either been in a private carriage, or she had walked in the company of others. Walking was preferable in that it was quicker, but from the carriage she had had more leisure to look around. When on foot, one had to be careful of where one stepped — and that was one thing, at least, that had not changed. There were still horses everywhere.

The locomotive drew into the station and great clouds of steam were pushed down from the high ceilings, swirling and eddying around. Cordelia and Ruby gathered their things together and in a few moments their door was swung open. A smartly dressed servant of the railways helped them down into a veritable maelstrom of noise and chaos.

"Where are all these people going, in such a rush, with such determined urgency?" Cordelia said.

"Like us, my lady, they are probably hungry and tired and simply want to be already arrived at their destination."

Cordelia was tall and she rose up onto the tips of her toes, hunting for Geoffrey, Stanley, Mrs Unsworth and Neville Fry. She was defeated by the sea of hats and pelisses and coats and cloaks. There was an abundance of colour, with the younger men favouring some positively alarming checked jackets, but the real peacocks were the older men who were clinging to the styles of the Regency and their youth. There was one gentleman who caught her eye and bowed low, and she laughed aloud at his red silk cravat, mustard yellow waistcoat, and bright blue coat.

"This way, my lady; I see them. We must find a cab to take us to the lodgings," Ruby urged.

Reality returned. Cordelia nodded. "We will perhaps need more than one carriage. These newer cabs are small, are they not? Let us go."

***

"I slept like a child!" Cordelia declared the next morning as she sat in a pleasant corner of a respectable and exclusive private dining room with smartly dressed waiting staff and a low buzz of educated conversation all around her. They were in an upstairs room close to Fleet Street.

Opposite her sat her literary agent, Septimus Gibbs. This selective eating house was a favourite haunt of his. He smiled. "You asked for lodgings somewhere both quiet and central, did you not?"

"You work miracles," she said. "The rooms are very modern and comfortable. I am in your debt, as always. I am confused, though. I thought that the Inns of Chancery were ancient institutions."

"They are. But you are in Furnival's Inn which was dissolved, oh I don't know when. Thirty years ago, perhaps? They pulled it down and rebuilt those apartments and lodgings there, in that clean, neo-classical way. Now, let me tell you the other reason I thought the place might suit you." Gibbs leaned forward. He was an angular man, but lean and ropey, like he was built from toughened oak and sinew. He was as white as snow, with dark eyes and very short grey hair which contrasted strangely with his still-black eyebrows. "Charles Dickens himself has lodged in those rooms, or some close to yours, I believe, at least in the same building."

"Goodness! I do hope his muse might rub off upon me."

"Ahh, my dearest friend, now we must talk about your column…"

She waved a heavy silver fork at him. "Not while we are eating kedgeree, Septimus."

He sat back again and dabbed at his mouth. "As you wish."

"However," she said, "You may tell me all that you know about this Louis Bonneville chap."

"Over kedgeree?"

"Please do."

"Well, then." And he began to explain that Bonneville was a politician of a rather reforming bent. He was part of the currently ruling Conservative Party, and a close supporter of the Prime Minister. Sir Robert Peel needed all the help he could get. The PM knew his tenure was coming to an end — it was his second time in the role, and he had been the incumbent for five years, this time around. Peel himself was a reformer and had been, according to Gibbs, stirring up much hatred on both sides of the House.

"They wonder who hates him more: the Whigs in opposition, or his own side. He's as likely to be stabbed in the back as by an opponent to his face," Gibbs said, shaking his head sadly.

"Oh. But you say that Bonneville was one of Peel's supporters...?"

"One of the few, yes, though it is said that Bonneville didn't think that Peel is going far enough with his reforms."

"And who supports, or sides with, this Bonneville?"

"I am not sure." Gibbs looked up and waved to a waiter to remove their empty plates. "I follow politics only as far as I need to; it's not the topic of *polite* conversation."

Cordelia reached across the table and patted his head. "But you make an exception for me."

"I make many exceptions for you, dear."

"Tell me about the murder. You must know more about that. It's far more exciting than politics."

"Exciting?"

"I am sorry," she said, and felt chastened immediately. "I realise it's hardly appropriate. But still. Humour my female weakness and lay out all the scandal for me."

Gibbs laughed. "You, female weakness? Well, well, you have changed since last I saw you. Ahh, the scandal is typically sordid. Are you sure?"

"Speak!"

"He was found dead in the arms of a prostitute in a cheap lodging house."

"Was she really a — girl of that nature, do you know?"

"Who, or what, else would she be?"

"Her father says she is not."

"Her father ... Cordelia, what are you not telling me? I am buying you breakfast. Don't reward me with duplicity."

"Septimus, of course I shan't. But the girl who has been arrested is the daughter of my butler."

"Is it still Mr Fry?"

"Indeed it is. And he is distraught."

"Goodness. I did not think the old goat to have been married. When did he ... but then the age of the girl ... I am confused."

"As well you might be." She sketched out the unfortunate circumstances, and Gibbs smiled.

"Well, well. And I would have placed bets that he was a confirmed bachelor."

"I suspect that his marriage was but a brief aberration." *As was mine*, she thought. "And so you must see that I have a connection to this matter."

Gibbs' smile faded. "You should be careful, Cordelia dear. Remember you are here in London on behalf of your column. There are some adjustments we need to make to your ... ah, style, and subject matter ... and it would not do for you to be running around after some murderess."

"She is not yet proven to be such!"

"Perhaps not."

"And I shall be having a cloak made!"

Gibbs blinked. "For…?"

"Me, as more appropriate *sleuthing* garb."

"Oh dear." Gibbs took her hands in his, and pressed firmly as he fixed her with his intense, dark stare. "I cannot tell you what to do, or what not to do. I have ever been a friend of your family, and I shall be for as long as I am on this earth. But do take care. This is London, and we have the new police now."

She gently withdrew her hands. "And that is why I am needed," she said, and began to take her leave.

***

When Cordelia got back to the lodgings, after a slow but uneventful ride in a slightly grubby hansom cab, she found Ruby quite alone in the comfortable sitting room with a stocking half-darned in her lap. She stood in a rush but Cordelia waved her back to her seat.

"I would not want to interrupt such uncommon industriousness," Cordelia said.

Ruby scowled at the darning. "Interruption would be welcome, my lady."

"Where is everyone?"

"Mr Fry has gone out on family business, but I know nothing more. He is too high to speak to the likes of me," Ruby said.

Cordelia stripped off her gloves and bonnet, and this time she allowed Ruby to jump up and begin to attend to her other outdoor garb.

Ruby continued to speak as she took the gloves and examined them for dirt and fraying. "Stanley is gone to church, and on a weekday too! He said he had to find the nearest place of worship so that he might rest more easily. Geoffrey has, likewise, gone to his own place of worship."

"An inn or alehouse."

"Just so. And as for Mrs Unsworth, well, who knows? She carries secrets with her. I, for one, would say that if groceries go missing, don't look to us. Look there."

"I am well aware that a certain amount of liberty is taken by *all* my staff," Cordelia said, and she glared hard at Ruby. "And I know all about the perks that are taken, and the percentages added by favouring one tradesman over another. But the unspoken agreement is that no one should overstep the mark."

"I do not think she can see the mark."

"Have you evidence?"

"None."

"Then speak no ill of her."

"But—"

"Enough. Anyway, I had given her orders to collect examples of unusual London street food and I have no doubt she is abroad on that very mission."

"And what of me, my lady?" Ruby said as petulance crept into her voice. "I have been quite trapped here."

"It would not do for you to run around alone out there," Cordelia said. "I think only of your safety."

"And you think that Stanley is more able to defend himself than I am?" Ruby sneered. "That lad would disarm an attacker by crumpling up and falling upon them."

Ruby had a point. The outspoken maid had shown herself more than capable of handling herself. Cordelia sighed. "We must be careful, Ruby. We are women alone in a great, dirty, hectic city."

"That's a good thing," Ruby said. "Now, tell me: what have you discovered about Bonneville?"

Cordelia relayed what Gibbs had just told her.

CHAPTER FIVE

It was some time later.

"These will surely kill you." Mrs Unsworth folded her flabby arms and stared at the ceramic bowl on the table.

Ruby had cleared a space around the bowl. Maid and mistress had been poring over newspapers in the sitting room, especially the Police Gazette, and making long lists of the friends and enemies of Bonneville, as far as they could determine from the strident editorials and vague allusions in the articles.

Then Mrs Unsworth had returned from her mission, and let an iron pot drop heavily onto a side dresser in the kitchen. "Eels, my lady. Street food, for you, as requested," she called through the door.

"Bring them here!"

And so Mrs Unsworth came through and deposited them on the table, stepped back, and made her solemn prediction. "You will be dead afore the morning," she said. "My lady."

Ruby was inclined to agree with the cook. "My lady, this is what the labourers eat. Not even I would stoop to eels."

Cordelia lifted the lid and peered at the pale gelatinous mass. The liquid was thin, and lumps broke the surface, glistening. The aroma was predominantly of vinegar with an undercurrent of nutmeg.

She held out her hand until Ruby pressed a spoon into it.

"Oh," said Cordelia after a moment's chewing. "It's not fishy at all. Are you sure you've bought eels, and not … something else?" Cat-meat was what people commonly expected to find in pies, it was said. "It's not too bad, you know. It's quite substantial. But the gravy is a poor thing. It seems to be simply flour and water, with spices."

Ruby peered more closely before straightening up and wrinkling her nose. "It's definitely eel, my lady. Ugh. What next? Oysters?"

"I suppose there is no chance of me gaining admittance to an oyster house," Cordelia said wistfully.

"My lady, without a man to chaperone you, you cannot eat anywhere in London, in public. And even accompanied, there are few places you can go."

"And yet you can be seen almost anywhere," Cordelia said sulkily. Then she shook herself. *Pouting would not brew the tea, would it,* she told herself firmly. "So it is. Standards, and all that. Mrs Unsworth, while you were on the streets, did you hear anything at all about the murder case?"

"Nothing," said the cook shortly. She stood by the door to the small kitchen, clearly waiting to be released back into her domain. Cordelia waved her away at last. It was very strange to have the kitchen so close to the general rooms for living. Cordelia was rather enjoying the informality of the lodgings. She wondered if it was similar to being on safari.

"There is nothing in the papers of any use," she said. "Save that many had taken against Bonneville, and cannot resist little digs even in his obituaries."

"There, then, are many suspects," Ruby said.

Cordelia looked at the list. "There's a dozen names here and not one of them convinces me that they would have enough cause to do the deed. And surely anyone who spoke out so boldly would not then kill him, would they? That would be a singularly stupid act."

"Murderers and criminals are stupid, my lady."

"Not so, and I think we would be wise not to underestimate this situation, Ruby. We are in London now, and things are very different here."

She realised she had said that, or thought that, many times lately. But people were the same, wherever they were; London contained the whole world in microcosm but was it so very different? People loved and fought and died, the same as anywhere else.

**

Shortly after the half-eaten eels were cleared away, Neville Fry entered the rooms. He had been assigned a small curtained-off area of the room where the men were sleeping, and in more usual circumstances, he would have been shocked and appalled that a butler was expected to share in such proximity to a coachman and his boy. Their place was the stables; although there were no stables handy. His place was far above the common servant.

Under the current cloud of murder and shame, however, he had barely seemed to register his unfavourable sleeping arrangements. He entered the main sitting room slowly, trying to keep himself professional and upright, but his thin face was drawn and looked many years older. Suddenly, nothing else mattered to him beyond family.

"I have been to visit Maisie," he announced.

Cordelia urged him to sit but he couldn't bring himself to do that. He remained by the door. "I thought your daughter was called Florence?"

"She is, my lady. Maisie is my, was my, well she is

Florence's mother."

Ah, his wife, she thought. *Still his wife yet, for he was hardly likely to have obtained an expensive divorce.* "And how is she?" Cordelia asked.

"Utterly distraught. But I have learned some things which may assist you when you go to speak to the policemen. She is being held in a police station house on Bow Street, as Florence put in her letter. Maisie has been to see her, and she could barely bring herself to speak of the conditions there!"

"And what of Florence herself?" Cordelia probed. "I appreciate that I may be speaking of indelicate things but do you know what brought your daughter and this politician together? Please do not be coy. Her very life may depend on your candour."

Fry nodded. "I understand. And I can assure you that she is a respectable girl ... though she may have undertaken a silly folly that shall certainly ruin her now! She was in the service of one man called Lord Brookfield, I understand."

"What, at the time of the murder? What manner of Lord? I am not sure that I have heard of him, I think. What is his full name, and his family?"

"I cannot say. All this is new to me. I asked my wife who it was that Florence presently worked for, and she went thin-lipped and then turned to crying. So perhaps Florence had been dismissed. But Maisie said that our daughter was a pure girl, a maiden, who had merely fallen into the clutches of this politician and she was no part of his murder, not at all."

She was not pure, not from the moment she fell into this man's clutches, Cordelia thought sadly. Ruby drew in a slow breath, loudly enough for Cordelia to hear, and she knew that her maid was signalling her, and she already knew what Ruby meant.

How pure, really? For though there were many men that drew women into their clutches, there were also women who would lay themselves out to be clutched upon.

She did not speak of that to the devastated father before her. "Can you tell me anything else?" she asked, as kindly as she could.

Fry shook his head. "Nothing that I think would be of use, my lady. Maisie was almost insensible at times. She says that the police in that division are corrupt, and cannot be trusted in anything."

Ruby snorted. "They all are, in every division."

Fry looked like he was soon to fall down if he did not sit down. Cordelia dismissed him. As soon as he had gone, she said to Ruby, "I must enter polite society at once. Or, at least, that portion that will still accept me."

"I am sure there will be many who shall not snub you.

Here in the city, there are few untouched by scandal, once one cares to dig."

"Of that I am sure. And speaking of such, what of this Lord Brookfield?"

"Do you know him, my lady?"

"I fear not. I suspect, however, that he is aristocracy, not merely gentility as I am." Cordelia's title was a courtesy one from her late husband. "But perhaps I have seen the name before. Something now tugs at my recollection." She grabbed the newspapers and unfolded the large, unwieldy sheets. "Ah, yes. There is simply a passing mention of his work in politics ..."

"Ah! So there is a connection, surely?" Ruby said.

"We are in the capital city, Ruby. Who here is not connected with one political party or another? He appears to be a Tory, like Peel himself, and Bonneville. So perhaps he is not a suspect ... indeed, as he is a Lord, I find that unlikely..."

Ruby laughed, then subsided as Cordelia gave her a stern look.

"At any rate," Cordelia continued, "he may know of Bonneville's enemies, and as he was Florence's master at some point, I ought to talk to this man. And if I were to attend some events, maybe some literary soirees, and the like, then I shall be able to talk to all manner of useful people. If not this particular Lord, then others."

"Mr Fry has asked you to talk to the police. And the police only."

Cordelia began to write a list. "And I shall, of course. Though I suspect we already both know what kind of reaction we're going to receive. They have their suspect, do they not? I know that I will be complicating matters for them."

"My lady, I foresee other problems here. If you enter society, and begin to ask questions, do you not think that this will alert the murderer, if indeed there is one, and it isn't poor Florence? And if the murderer is alerted, what then? He will run to cover. Furthermore, my lady, your exploits in Cambridgeshire and Yorkshire are becoming known. If you ask questions, it will be obvious to all that you are trying to set up as some kind of Lady Detective."

Cordelia smiled, liking that description. Ruby sighed. "You may hamper the investigation, my lady."

"What investigation? The police are done with it already. No, if the murderer be cunning, then I shall be more cunning still. We women are bred to it, are we not?"

"And yet," Ruby said, "this murderer is already ahead of you."

"How so?"

"He knows what you do not."

CHAPTER SIX

Cordelia intended to get into society, and she managed it. In a country town, she would have been invited to At Homes and Luncheons, but the city was such a roiling mass of coming and going that one had to stand up and shout to be noticed. Stanley was fairly exhausted with the flurry of messages he was tasked with conveying about London. Within a day or two, she had managed to get herself invited — courtesy of her agent, Gibbs and his long-reaching influence — to a literary soiree. Being a matter of the Arts, it had a rather more liberal air to it than some other places. And it was a situation that brought together those with similar interests rather than just similar accidents of birth. Not that it was quite as liberal as to admit tradesmen and the like, but it had a daringly European feel to the mix of guests.

She had not heard that the intriguing Lord Brookfield

would be there, but she felt that any connections she began to make would be useful. After her marriage, some of her old contacts had fallen away. A widow was tainted, in some way. It was time to make new friends.

Gibbs accompanied her as she could hardly attend the gathering alone. She was supremely grateful to him for taking the time out of his busy schedule, but he was a true gentleman and assured her that the pleasure was all his.

"Besides," he said, "this is also my job; to see and be seen in such places. Indeed, you are merely making my tedious role slightly more bearable. It is I who am grateful to you. Here, now; let me introduce you to Mrs Hunter-Jenkinson and the Colonel himself."

Cordelia smiled warmly as Gibbs led her around the small gathering in the hired assembly rooms, which had been decked out in classic gold and cream. Her smile, however, soon faded from warm to coldly forced. She was not received with as much glory as she was expecting. Her conversation with Delilah Fotheringhay was typical of her interactions.

"Somebody suggested that you ... *wrote*," the woman said. She was in her late twenties, with a beautiful heart-shaped face, large dark eyes, and a tiny rosebud mouth that was currently pinched up into an expression of disgust, as if Cordelia still smelled of eels and oysters.

46

"I am currently the weekly cookery correspondent in a household magazine!" Cordelia said. She'd been trying out a number of different ways to describe herself. "Correspondent" had a glamorous and slightly daring ring to it, she thought.

"Cookery? You write about being a *cook*?" Delilah said, dropping her voice and taking a step back. Clearly she didn't want anyone to know what sort of woman she was associating with.

"I am not a cook. I am Cordelia, Lady Cornbrook," she reminded her. Gibbs had made the introduction, of course, before fading away to speak with someone else. "I take an academic interest in the culinary arts and their varied and complex histories," Cordelia said, somehow managing to retain her smile.

The rosebud mouth of Delilah seemed to purse up even more. Her pale face was almost the same colour as the satiny wallpaper behind her and she seemed to blanch even further at Cordelia's words. "Goodness me," she said, in the same tone that her coachman Geoffrey would utter something much more earthy. "An academic interest, you say. How frightfully ... *different.*"

Different. Dilettante. Potentially dangerous. "Of course," Cordelia said, finally letting her smile fade. "I am not the only one to do so. Many ladies are taking it upon themselves to instruct their fellows and the lesser ranks. It is quite the new thing. And a good thing, too. For without difference and change, we would have no progress."

"As if progress is a *good* thing," Delilah said sniffily. "Any student of history could tell you that the relentless march of *progress* is destroying our once-proud nation."

Cordelia reminded herself that she did not know Delilah, and that Delilah did not know her. An argument here would be both inelegant and potentially damaging to her reputation. Were she a man, she could have engaged in a hearty debate and that would have done nothing but proved her prowess; as a woman she had to bite back her retorts. She certainly wasn't going to summon up a smile again, though. She was about to trot out a polite excuse and take her leave, when a couple approached, and greeted Delilah so that she was forced then to introduce Cordelia to them.

Mr Anthony Delaney turned out to be a stipendiary magistrate of some gravity, with close-cropped metal-grey hair and a narrow, yellow face. In contrast to his severity, his wife was younger, warmer and loquacious. She was only slightly shorter than her husband, and stood with a hunch, making Cordelia wonder if she deliberately tried to seem smaller than her man. She appeared utterly devoted to him, and the only time that Mr Delaney smiled was when he was addressing "my darling Ivy." And to Ivy, he was "my Anthony."

"I think progress is utterly wonderful!" Ivy was gushing as the unpleasant Delilah sidled away. After a few polite remarks, Mr Delaney allowed himself to be drawn into a nearby conversation about the Americas, leaving Cordelia quite alone with Ivy and her hyperbole.

"Indeed, I agree," Cordelia murmured. She noticed that there was a large circle of emptiness around them, in contrast to the heaving throng in other parts of the room.

Ivy warbled on. "Of course, London is growing so fast now; I've always lived here and I barely recognise the streets of my childhood and yes, of course, that could be disconcerting but really, don't you think, it's just one small price to pay for the marvellous future we are building?"

"Yes, no, yes, rather."

Ivy, to her credit, slowed down, and asked Cordelia about her own childhood. She listened intently, nodding, and appeared to be actually taking everything in. She made all the right comments about the right things at the right time, and Cordelia was convinced that Ivy was genuinely lovely.

It was somewhat unsettling. Her thoughts wandered. *Most people have an ulterior motive, don't they?* Even Cordelia did.

"…and the telegraph!" Ivy saying and it jerked Cordelia back to the conversation. "Do you not remember that ghastly murder? Poor Sarah Hart! Poisoned!"

"It was a Quaker that did it, was it not?" Cordelia said. The dreadful events had dominated the news the previous year, even overshadowing Cordelia's own exploits. The shocking murder at Slough just proved, to Cordelia, that no matter one's background or apparent appearance to the world at large, even if one was a strictly religious man, you never really knew what someone was capable of.

"He was, yes, a Quaker, of course; though they have denied that he is one of their own, certainly since the murder, and who can blame them, of course. Of course. And caught by the electric telegraph! Now, does that not just seal everything we have seen saying about the wonderful march of progress? Justice, wrought real by progress, indeed!"

"Indeed," Cordelia agreed weakly. She was scanning the room now, looking for escape. Ivy caught her look, and misinterpreted it. She hooked her arm into Cordelia's, an overly familiar gesture that should have earned her a reprimand, and began to steer them both in the direction of more drinks.

Cordelia dearly wanted to speak to other people, but Ivy was an unstoppable force, and her conversation was interesting, if a little dominating. Over the course of the next few glasses of alcohol, Cordelia told Ivy all about her writing, and Ivy told her far more than Cordelia wanted to know about the life of a sitting magistrate at Bow Street, the toll roads, how the new haberdasher near to her townhouse was bringing in new silks, what type of cake she preferred to eat, and why she thought that lupins were a most delightful flower.

By the time that Cordelia was rescued by Gibbs, she was very drunk indeed, and Ivy didn't seem at all affected by the alcohol. Her husband towed her away, and she went willingly, waving enthusiastically at Cordelia the whole time. "I shall call!" she trilled as she was engulfed by the crowd.

Cordelia felt delight and dread in equal measure, and felt like a bad person for it.

CHAPTER SEVEN

Cordelia had expected to have a hangover the next morning, but she did not expect to find that Ruby had one, also. Mistress and servant blinked at one another in the artificial gloom of the kitchen, while Mrs Unsworth fretted by the stove and muttered about the blinds being lowered during the day, marking them as classless people. She had spread a white cloth on the table because of Cordelia's appearance. "I have no girl to help me," she said in her continuing list of complaints. "The table needs scrubbing, and there is no Calais sand, and who is to bake the breakfast rolls?"

"Send Stanley out to buy some," Cordelia said. "That is what they do here. As Ruby told me, no one cooks in London."

Mrs Unsworth huffed her way out of the room. "As good as telling me I'm useless..." was her muttered parting shot.

Cordelia looked at Ruby, who slid onto the bench by the table and groaned as she did so.

"I did not give you permission to go out last night," Cordelia said, in between mouthfuls of watery and suspiciously grey milk. But then, she had seen no cows in London. *How did it get to the city? How did it stay fresh? Though this was not "fresh."*

"No, my lady, for I quite forgot to ask for permission until it was too late, and you had already left for your engagement." Ruby tried to look contrite but she mostly looked ill. "Anyway, there was no harm done."

"Except to your head, it seems. Have we any of Mr Peeble's Salts?"

Ruby grunted, stood up, and went slowly about her task.

***

Later, once Cordelia was better able to tolerate bright lights and noise, she took Stanley as her chaperone to the police station house where Florence was being held in custody. She felt better with a man at her side, though Stanley was but an overgrown streak of a boy. Women were walking freely about the city streets, but the better-dressed sort would stay in pairs or groups. The only lone women were poor ones. If a solitary woman appeared finely dressed, one could easily guess — or, perhaps, assume — as to her occupation.

The station house was small and shabby, and she was surprised. All the fanfare about the new police had led her to think that they would be housed in fine barracks of some kind. Instead, she found herself in a dirty street, crowded all about by every section of low society, and she drew herself closer to Stanley as they stood opposite the steps and looked towards the entrance.

"What do you suppose that policeman is doing?" she said. "Is he arresting that poor unfortunate woman?"

"My lady," Stanley said, his stammer bad in the stress of the London surroundings, "I fear he is handing her money."

"As charity?" Cordelia said, suspicion immediately rising in her.

"Er…"

The blue-coated Peeler then took the shabby woman's arm and led her away, whereupon they disappeared together into an alleyway.

"I should not be shocked," Cordelia said. "Such lowly transactions occur by the minute in this city. And yet…"

"Quite so, my lady," Stanley said. "Sin."

It wasn't the sin so much as the parties indulging in it, she thought. A policeman, who ought to be against all manner of vice, here in plain sight encouraging it. Grimly, she started forward for the steps up to the main door of the station house, and Stanley scampered alongside.

She was met as soon as she entered the dark lobby. A man with unruly dark whiskers and badly-shaved stubble about his chin loomed large in front of her, and spoke directly to Stanley.

"Your business here, boy?"

Stanley gurgled and coughed, and turned to Cordelia. "My mistress, ah, Lady Cornbrook..." was all he managed to say.

The policeman glanced at Cordelia. His tall top hat, dented at the crown where the iron ring that strengthened it had clearly taken a blow, remained on his head. In fact he made no move at all to acknowledge her status. "And your business?" he repeated.

Cordelia said, "We are here to see Florence Fry."

The policeman shrugged. "As to that, I must say no. Good day to you."

"You do not understand!" Cordelia insisted, stepping forward. "Look here. Her father is my butler, and there is great doubt as to the poor girl's guilt. I am not here on a social call, nor am I one of those ghouls who like to visit the condemned. No, I am here in the name of justice. You cannot prevent me from seeing her."

"I can," the man said. He stared at her, making his boredom plain through his half-stifled yawn and slitted eyes.

What was Cordelia to do? She could hardly rush herself at the man, bodily throwing him aside. And she had no influence here, and no friends to call upon, nor even any threats she could make.

Infuriated and frustrated, she retreated with Stanley, almost trembling with impotent fury.

"How dare he!" she exploded as they drew themselves away from the busy thoroughfares and took shelter against the wall of a respectable-looking shop.

Stanley looked as angry as his long face would allow. He stared away for a moment, deep in thought. Then he surprised Cordelia by saying, "My lady, if I may ... do you wait here in this draper's shop and I shall be back as soon as I may." He hardly stammered at all, distracted as he was by his plans.

Amazed by his order, she did as he bid her. She entered the well-lit shop while Stanley disappeared on his curious mission.

By the time that he returned she had already ordered a quantity of thin but warm woollen cloth to be made up into a cloak, with a wide shoulder cape and slits for the arms, in the latest style. Stanley poked his head into the shop and beckoned her out onto the street.

She opened her mouth to greet him, and promptly shut it again when she saw that they had company.

"Cordelia, Lady Cornbrook," he said. "And this is the Reverend Albert Griffin. I met him yesterday when I was going round and about to find a place to worship."

"How do you do," they said to one another. He was a young man of the cloth, and had bulging eyes and a wide, likeable smile.

"So," he said, in a strong local accent, "we are to gain access to the cells in the station house, are we? Tis a place very familiar to me, I must say. As our Lord and Saviour himself often…"

He burbled away happily, almost like a light and innocent child as he led them back to the station house. But his stride, Cordelia noticed, was in complete opposition to his frothy words. He walked like a man marching into battle, and he held his head like the general of an army.

He was not going to be turned away; not easily.

He surged into the lobby, still nattering about the good deeds of various saints, and accosted the same policeman that had turned Cordelia and Stanley away.

"Good day! How goes things today, Mr Lyons? A grand day for it, a grand day indeed. Inspector Hood is about, is he not? I fancy I did see him earlier. I will just say hello to him on my way to the cells."

"Sir, I think that … I mean, these persons with you …"

"Yes, yes, I shall introduce them to the Inspector too, you may have no fear — aha! And there he is, the man himself, well how delightful to see you. Inspector! Here we have the esteemed Lady Cornbrook and her right-hand man, Mr Stanley Ashdown. We are on our way to save the soul, if we might, of one of your latest unfortunate residents, the poor Miss Fry. Which cell, if you please?"

Inspector Hood, who had eyes to match his surname, glowered at them all, but he was powerless against the man of the cloth, especially in such a public place. The lobby was full of people crowding up to the front desk, coming in and out of doors, and peering around corners. Hood waved them all towards a small door at the back of the room, which was wedged open with a broken chair.

Cordelia walked very tall as she swept past all the staring, angry eyes of the policemen. They would remember her, she was sure of it. Was that good or bad?

She did not really want to make enemies, especially of those in authority.

Inspector Hood hissed like a snake as she went by.

CHAPTER EIGHT

The reverend insisted on remaining with Cordelia and Stanley, and she could hardly turn him away. In truth, as she stepped along the corridor in the very bowels of the police station house, she was grateful for his comforting presence to her left shoulder. It was cold and dark and damp, exactly as she had imagined a prison to be. The corridor was narrow, and badly lit. Could they not afford lamps? She had expected it to smell bad, but imagination is one thing and the reality something quite other. In this case, the reality was much worse. The smell had the sharp tang of stale urine mixed with an earthiness which she supposed was from the floor and walls. There was a rankness of sweat, and it was tinged with the flavour of the sickroom. She tried not to breathe too deeply.

Above all else, though, she was surprised by the noise. The corridor had open-barred cells to either side, and each one housed a crowd of men — and women. In many cases the occupants were, to Cordelia's mind, simply children. *But children can be as corrupt as any adult,* she reminded herself. She had read a study that suggested that more of their character was due to nurture, and their upbringing, than their innate nature and position of birth, but that would blame their families and society and such a conclusion would lead to some difficult questions. So she tried not to look at the large-eyed youngsters that reached out their bony sparrow hands to clutch at her clothing as she passed by. The reverend and Stanley kept to each side of her and preventing them from touching her.

They called and they booed, both adult and child alike; they whistled and they shouted and they catcalled. They grunted at one another and there was a perpetual clanging of metal on metal, dully echoing through the badly lit passageway.

"This is not even a true prison," the reverend said, as he caught up to Cordelia's side and saw her face. "They will be before the police magistrates soon enough, and sentenced, and moved on. This is a holding facility, in truth, and nothing more."

"So there is no need for any comforts," she replied.

"Nor is it any better in prison proper, nor on a transport ship," the reverend said. "I work often in such places and ..." But he tailed off, his former buoyancy quite dampened down by his surroundings. "Ah, here we are."

The cells were smaller at this end, and more sparsely occupied. They came to one windowless cube that housed only one person, a tall woman all folded in on herself as she curled on a rough mattress on a low wooden bench. She looked up as the three of them stopped by the bars. Cordelia felt uncomfortable. Was there no privacy at all in such a place?

"Miss Fry?" Reverend Griffin said, his voice now low and kind.

"Who asks?" she retorted, oblivious to his black and sober clothing.

"I am Cordelia, Lady Cornbrook," Cordelia said before Reverend Griffin could speak. "And your father has asked for our assistance in your present predicament. May we come in?"

"I cannot stop you," the girl said diffidently.

Cordelia hesitated.

"Please," Florence said, her tone softening. "I am sorry, my lady. Forgive me." She struggled to her feet and smoothed her dress down. "I have been many nights in this place, and I've got some rougher edges from those around me. It's like an infection, my lady. I've even got to talking a little rougher."

Her accent was already of the streets, Cordelia noticed; she was a London girl, through and through, dropping the 'h' from some words and adding them on, quite superfluously, to others. The reverend waved at a policeman who was at the far end of the corridor, and he came to unlock the heavy door. "Watch her, all right?" the policeman said, and let them in.

Cordelia shook Florence's thin hand. She had the high-chinned air of her father about her, but more rounded facial features. Even in the gloom of the cell, she was beautiful, though that impression came at least half from her youthfulness.

And she batted her eyelashes at both Stanley and the reverend, and turned only at the last to Cordelia. "My lady, I'd offer you a seat but as you can see..." She waved her arm around the room.

"I am well able to stand. Now, Florence, you must have no fear in speaking the plain truth to me, however unsavoury some elements of it might be. Tell me all about Louis Bonneville. And I do mean *all*."

"Unsavoury?" Florence half-closed her eyes and smiled in a secret little way. "Oh, no, my lady, there is nothing at all unsavoury to tell you. We were in love, and everyone knows that love is the most beautiful and pure thing there is." She then stifled a sob and pressed her hand to her mouth. "Of course, he is dead now, and I ought to be in mourning, but here I am..." She half turned away.

"Mourning?" Cordelia said sharply. "Why, had you and he ... in secret, had you married?"

"Oh, no, my lady," Florence said. "We would have, in time, I am sure of it. But we were two hearts wed together as surely as any married couple."

Good heavens, are you thirteen? Cordelia thought. She kept that comment to herself and instead mustered some sympathy for the poor lost girl. "And who else knew of your love?" she asked.

Florence hung her head and sighed heavily. She folded her arms, then unfolded them, then rubbed at her face, and finally she answered. "We could meet only in secret," she confessed. "No one else knew, due to his station and my own. And yet there are cases of high born men marrying their servants, aren't there? I have read about it. We could be such. We could have been such."

"And this was definitely love and not..." Cordelia said.

"And not *business,* no!" Florence threw her head back and her dark eyes were rimmed with tears, making them sparkle in the shadows of her face. "And anyone who says that is a lowly cur who deserves to die in a ditch!"

Those harsh words from the pretty woman shocked Stanley; Cordelia could feel his horror as he went rigid and held his breath. The reverend, as a man who worked with all people, did not murmur or make any surprised sound.

"Thank you for confirming that," Cordelia said mildly, unimpressed by Florence's display. "And now another question, if I may. You protest your innocence, of course?"

"Of course!"

"And so then we must ask, why is it that you are here?"

"I have been framed! Someone's got it in for me, they have." Her accent was rougher by the minute.

Cordelia knew her next question would provoke more anger. "And yet who would go to the effort of framing you?"

Florence clenched her fists.

And then she burst into tears. She wasn't stifling her sobs any longer; she wailed and screamed like a toddler. Even the reverend was moved to reach out his hand and place it on her upper arm, but she wrenched it away, and said, "Yes, who would frame *me?* A nobody, a minnow, a meaningless waif. A fatherless wretch. Even my own mother said as much. I am nothing to nobody and so, then, why me? I don't know! I don't know! Why would *I* know?"

Cordelia waited. Reverend Griffin cleared his throat as if to speak but Cordelia put her hand out in a warning gesture, and he caught the meaning, and sealed his lips. He, too, must have used the technique of silence, allowing the other person the time to form their thoughts without pressure or hurry.

It worked, as it almost always did. Florence gathered her composure, shaky though it was, and eventually she could talk again. "I know why they think I'm a nobody," she said. "I know why they can't understand why anyone would even want to love me. They don't believe that a good, strong man like Louis could fall for someone like me, so they don't want to look for the truth, do they?"

"Someone like you...?" Cordelia prompted.

Florence let her arms rise and fall to her sides.

Cordelia changed tack. Something had been on her mind. "Florence, do you still work for Lord Brookfield?"

Florence blinked a few times, clearing her eyes of unshed tears. "Oh, no, my lady, I don't. I left His Lordship's service some time ago."

"To do what?"

"Oh, I suppose that you think I went to become a kept woman of Louis, don't you?" Florence said, her belligerence rising once more.

"I suppose nothing. I seek only the truth, without judgement," she replied.

"Well, then, judge this," Florence said bitterly. "I was passed from that Lord Brookfield to one Mr Albert Socks. And yes, as a kept woman."

"And were you originally... kept ... by Lord Brookfield?"

Florence was facing the wall by this point, presenting her back to them all as she stared up at nothing. "The Right Honourable Lord Brookfield was ever kind to me, and a good man, gentle and decent," she said. "Old-fashioned."

"And can you say the same for this Albert Socks?"

Florence shrugged. "He was a master like any other," she commented.

"So the Lord Brookfield and Mr Socks are friends?"

"They are contemporaries in the political world. I don't claim to understand a word of all that."

"And were either man connected with Louis Bonneville?"

"Mr Socks and Louis, yes."

"As friends? Will these men, the Lord Brookfield and Mr Socks, be in a state of distress at their colleague's demise?"

"Perhaps. It's the world of men and power. What do I know? I just gave Louis solace. It was a hard path that he walked. He had principles, my lady. True principles. We would meet and he would be so full of anger and stress but my job was always as helpmeet. I strove to ease the burden from his shoulders. I am sure your clergyman there can understand that."

Cordelia listened intently and picked up on one thing in Florence's words. "And where, exactly, did you habitually meet?"

"The room he was murdered in!" That provoked a few fresh sobs.

"And this was in a lodging house, was it?"

"Mrs Clancey's," Florence said. "It was he that got me the room and the key for it, though he would use it himself also. There were some times that I could not go…"

Reverend Griffin cleared his throat and moved in closer to Cordelia to whisper into her ear. "My lady, I hate to hurry you along in this vital work but my congregation will be awaiting me."

Cordelia nodded. "What times could you not go?" she asked.

Florence shook her head. "Just a few times, when he asked me to stay at his house instead."

"His house? You went to Bonneville's house?"

"No, my lady, I have never been to my Louis's house. No, I mean that it was Mr Socks, Mr Albert Socks, who got me the key to the lodging house."

"Why? Did he know about you and Mr Bonneville? You just said that it was a secret."

"No, he had no idea about the extent of our love, or anything. He just knew I needed somewhere to go, that was all. Somewhere to be free."

Somewhere to make money lying down, Cordelia thought. What did Socks mean by giving his own woman, his maidservant-with-extras, the key to a room elsewhere, when she lived at his house? She was aware of Reverend Griffin waiting for her to finish. She quickly ran through everything they had discussed. Was there anything else she had missed?

Her ruminations were interrupted by a shout from outside. It echoed down the corridor. "Your time is up, sir!" Inspector Hood could clearly contain himself no longer and he appeared at the barred gate. "I have bent to your will for as long as I am able, sir!"

"Thank you, and it is most appreciated." Reverend Griffin bowed to Florence and then hustled Stanley and Cordelia from the cell. She barely had time to murmur her appreciation before he had taken his leave of them on the front steps of the station house, urging Stanley to take good care of Cordelia, and for Cordelia herself to take good care of her own soul.

"I should have asked her who she thought would kill Bonneville," she remarked to Stanley as he began to look around for a cab to take them back to their rooms.

"I don't think she would have known," Stanley said. "It was a disagreeable place, and she..."

"Yes, I know. She was a disagreeable woman. And yet,

in her position, would we not act the same?" *Maybe it was more nurture and not nature,* she thought, trying to picture herself as a poor woman with no means and no friends, falling in with a rich and powerful politician. *What morals would I happily put to one side, if I thought there was love, or money, or safety, in it?*

CHAPTER NINE

"Mr Neville Fry!" Cordelia called as she re-entered her rented rooms at the Inns of Court. Her tone was just one notch below "shouting" and a good few above what her tutors would have called "ladylike."

Neville emerged hastily from the kitchen. His sleeves were covered by long protectors and his hands were blackened from polishing the silverware that they had brought with them in a wicker basket. He had a large apron over his usual sombre suit. "My lady?"

"We've been to see your daughter," she said, flopping into a chair as Ruby scurried forward to take her hat and gloves. "Stanley, ask Mrs Unsworth to brew me up a refreshing pot of tea. Make it strong; I can still taste the air of the cells. Ruby, if you would serve when it is ready. Now, Mr Fry, do sit. Please," she said again as he reluctantly hovered by the door. "This may take some time. *Sit.*"

He perched, ram-rod straight, deeply uncomfortable in his working clothes. But he was keen — indeed, desperate — to hear news of his daughter. His paternal love overrode any societal mores.

Cordelia wanted to kick off her outdoor shoes but she couldn't do that in front of Neville. She sat alongside a table and twisted; her skirts were too large, with their layers of starched petticoats, to be able to tuck underneath the low table comfortably. Various notebooks and papers were already scattered around, just like in her study at home. She pulled one notebook towards her and took up a pencil.

"Have you heard of Albert Socks?" she said.

"No. How is she, my Florence? You said you saw her; did you actually speak to her? Oh, my lady, I am sorry to bombard you but my heart aches. Did she ask after me?"

She did not, Cordelia noted. *She actually called herself fatherless.* "I spoke with her at length," she said, "and she is in good health, as far as I can tell. Albert Socks is, or perhaps was, her employer." She wondered how to broach the reality of the situation, as far as she could tell. "She was employed as … as his … companion, in a sense."

"No. Never! She was a good maidservant." His face showed that he understood what Cordelia implied, and that he was horrified by it. "There must be a misunderstanding. She would have been a maid."

"A maid of some status. And previously she had performed the same role for the Lord Brookfield."

"And do you mean to say that she ... with this Bonneville also..."

"No, not at all," she said. "I hope that you might find some comfort in this but she declared nothing but love for Bonneville. She spoke of him as a lover. Her *only* lover."

"Comfort? Forgive me, my lady, I see no comfort in this. She was unwed! She had no business taking a lover."

"But you must see, surely, that it is good that she was not with Bonneville under coercion or any such thing. Just from a pure motive of her heart."

"My lady, she was unmarried and everything you speak of is impure. Wrong!" He shook his head dejectedly and fixed his gaze across the room. She could see the emotions warring within him; love for his daughter and hate for the situation that had ruined her. For that, his daughter had to take some blame. *It is always the way,* Cordelia thought. *We must be angels but if we fall, we are at fault, not the ones who put us up so high that we could not fail to fall.*

She moved the subject away from Florence. "Albert Socks is also a political man," she said. "What do you know of this world?"

"I? But I am a butler, my lady. Do you not know more than I ever could?"

"I have no connections, either. This is a section of society unknown to me. I have heard of wild parties, and secret pacts, and blackmail and business and money, which makes anyone quite irrational."

"There would be no wild parties for my Florence," Neville said. "She does not touch a drop of any alcohol."

Cordelia's condescending scepticism was impossible to hide from her face. She knew Neville could see it when he said, before she could reply, "My lady, it is true. It is one thing that both I and her mother can be proud of her for. Although perhaps that 'proud' is not quite correct. Actually, it is her lack of stomach for the stuff that prevents her from drinking, rather than any morality and strength on her part."

"She does not handle her drink, or has a delicate head the next day?"

"Oh, it is far more than that, my lady. Indeed, her body rejects it all most violently and almost instantly!"

"Interesting. Oh, Ruby, the tea; just place the tray here. Please, do stay. I will wish to talk this over with you anyway."

Ruby did not need cajoling to sit down. At the barest hint from Cordelia, she had pulled up a comfortable chair and was less hampered than her mistress by voluminous skirts. She did stop short of helping herself to a cup of tea, of course. Neville was already incandescent at the impropriety of Ruby *sitting* right there, in the same room as her mistress. Ruby waited as Cordelia took a sip of tea and declared it delicious.

"Now then," Cordelia continued. "So I wonder, what is this connection between Louis Bonneville and Albert Socks? Both are politicians. I must write this down." She spoke aloud as she wrote, trying to remember everything that Florence had told her in the cell. "So, Lord Brookfield gave her to Albert Socks. So they can be assumed to be friends. And she said they would know Bonneville, and that would be fair enough as all move in the same circles, it would seem. And yet…"

"But you are saying that all politicians are linked to all others, my lady," Ruby said. "I am a maid yet I am not intimately acquainted with all other maids here."

No, just all the footmen with their well-turned calves, Cordelia thought. She suppressed her smile. "Something is nagging at my mind," she said. She leaned against the table with her elbow, and a newspaper caught her eye. "Yes, here," she said, and began to unfold the unwieldly thing. "Why do they have to make these things so blasted large?" she muttered. "Ah, I have it."

"What, my lady?" both Ruby and Neville said.

"Here it is, in the gossip section. Socks and Brookfield had snubbed one another at a shoot. Red stags, just last month, at the end of the season for such things."

"Really?"

Cordelia passed the newspaper to Ruby, who squinted at the close-packed print. "I do not see it."

Cordelia took it back and read the snippet aloud. "We hear that the Lord B——, that politician so close to our PM, and lately come in from a watery pasture, has decidedly turned his nose up at one particular Article of Footwear."

Neville and Ruby looked at one another.

"No, I am not run quite mad," Cordelia said, "and you need not collude between yourselves to send for the head-doctor. It is in code, just like a riddle. It's very mode, you know. Lord B is clearly Lord Brookfield — watery pasture, obviously. And the article of footwear must be Socks."

"Or a man named Boot?"

"I don't know any men named Boot."

"You didn't know Socks, either, my lady," Ruby said.

"I will concede that it is a stretch. Nevertheless…" Cordelia carefully snipped the fragment from the paper with a small pair of decoupage scissors. "It could also be a clue. They are suspects, to my mind, for they are connected, and they will be connected to the murder, I am sure of it. And if they are not, then they are starting pieces. These first people mark the ends of the thread and I must tug at them to see what unravels."

"All these allusions and codes and riddles make my head hurt," Ruby said.

"That will be the drink from last night," Cordelia said. "I do fear for your constitution, my dear girl. Anyway. Here we have a starting list of suspects." She scribbled furiously.

"My lady, look to the premises," Ruby said. Neville was a quiet spectator as the two women batted ideas at one another. "This lodging house that you spoke of. What of it? Where is it? Do you not find it odd that Socks had given Florence a key?"

"I do," Cordelia said, and made another note.

"Furthermore," Ruby went on, "look less to Bonneville's connections and friends. What of his enemies? They are more likely to kill him."

Cordelia unearthed another list she had made. "I already have. I have compiled this list of names from the newspapers and periodicals. Here are all the people who have railed against Bonneville's politics and ideas. The problem is, alas, that in politics and government matters, two men can be sworn enemies one day and the best of friends the next, depending on what policy needs decrying or supporting. It is an awfully long list."

"More than that," Ruby said. "For half the time, these friends are but sham friends, and these enemies are enemies only for show, I think."

"Still, it is all we have at the moment. We must get out there and meet these people, face to face, and discover which of them are true enemies. Ruby, I have a task for you." Cordelia pushed the list of Bonneville's enemies across to her maid. "Get you to Socks' house; talk to the staff and see if anyone mentions any of these people. Follow any trail at all that leads to Bonneville."

"And where is Socks' house?"

"I do not know, but nothing is truly secret in this city. He is a politician, and will be known. You must ask on the streets and I shall ask in my circles."

"You have no circles here," Ruby said.

Cordelia pursed her lips.

Ruby said, hastily, "My lady, I mean—"

"I know, I know. It is what it is. I shall go to Gibbs, for he shall be my way to the Lord Brookfield. He got me admitted to that soiree. He will get me to other places. We must also ask ourselves, always, who has benefited from the death of this man?"

"Not my daughter, that is for sure," Neville Fry said at last.

Cordelia wondered at that. Privately, there could be a thousand reasons why Florence would want the man dead but if so, she was faking her grief rather well, in spite of her flashes of anger.

"But you cannot go alone," Cordelia said as Ruby stood up. "Take Stanley with you for protection. And no, do not say it. I know what you might think of him. But the lad is resourceful and has proved himself to me on more than one occasion, as you well know."

"In many ways he has, my lady," Ruby conceded. "And yet on the rough streets...?"

"Well, before you go, speak to Geoffrey and ask him."

"For...?"

"For anything that he feels you might find useful for your defence."

Ruby nearly rolled her eyes. She nodded, and departed.

Neville, who had not witnessed the shocking lack of propriety between mistress and servant to this degree before, was slack-jawed with amazement. He stumbled to his feet and was wordless in his retreat.

CHAPTER TEN

Cordelia asked Geoffrey to accompany her to Septimus Gibbs' offices. He smartened himself up as much as he was able, and terrified the Hansom cab driver so much that they were woefully undercharged for the journey. It was a short one, anyway, just to the south of where they were.

Gibbs had his offices a few streets behind Fleet Street. She left Geoffrey mooching around in the street, glowering at people. She was greeted in the lobby by an over-attentive and odious-smelling man in a garish gilt-edged dark navy blue jacket that reached the middle of his calves. He oozed up the stairs, holding her arm, and rapped on Gibbs' office door. She paid him to go away.

"Come!" Gibbs barked from within, and when she opened the door, his beetle-black eyebrows shot up. "Cordelia! What on earth brings you here?"

"My dear Septimus. I believe you had some advice to

impart to me on the matter of my cookery column, and we never did get to discuss it."

"My main advice would be to not miss a deadline," he said, coming around the desk to press her hands in his. "I dined last night with the editor, and he tells me that your copy has not been delivered. They cannot hold the press, you know. The next edition will not have your work in it. I assured him you were a professional…"

"Oh, I am so sorry. I have half-written it. I need to obtain more information about Billingsgate."

"And that brings me to my second advice … don't go to Billingsgate."

"But it is a wondrous fish market!"

"It is a fish market but as to 'wondrous', I would disagree. 'Malodorous' and 'highly inappropriate for a lady' though." He sighed. "Please, do sit. I will not hedge my words. Cordelia, you must change the thrust of your articles. They lack refinement. They are not what people expect from a lady."

They argued lightly for a few minutes. She was quite put out about the whole affair. "I am writing what I, myself, would like to read!"

"Sadly, you are a singular woman," he insisted. "You think and act differently to the masses."

"I think and act as I please, and most do not."

"True. I hesitate to cast judgement as to whether that's a good thing. Please, think on my words. I fear your column will not last long if the editor keeps receiving complaints."

She flared her nostrils and waved her hand dismissively although she knew such arrogance would not make any impression on Gibbs. "Well, it is not the main reason I am here to see you, anyway."

"I thought not."

"I need to meet the Lord Brookfield."

"Ah, that politician?"

"The same. Who is he?"

"Charles Alfred Stone, the fourth Baron Brookfield. I do not mix in his circles, my dear."

"You have more chance of it than I do, though. Please, Septimus. It really is a matter of life and death. It is beyond frustrating that I cannot move about London as I wish to, and nor can I send my servants into the sorts of clubs that this lord will go. Only you can help me."

"Only I? I am flattered. This is all about that murder, then?"

"It is." She told him about her experience at the police station house and he shook his head, just a slight hint of amusement on his face.

"You must be careful, Cordelia. That particular division is a corrupt one; more corrupt than the others.

Remember that such corruption festers down from above as much as from below. Men do not last long there, unless they can embrace bribery and blackmail, or so it is said. Certainly that division has too many cases of men being sacked for misconduct."

"I suspected as much. I saw a lot to disturb me there."

"Tread lightly. Concentrate on your column. And if you can rein in your more earthy tendencies, then I shall forge out and seek this Lord Brookfield for you."

He stood up and she rose as well. He shook her hand and held it, warmly.

"Thank you, Septimus. You have ever been good to me."

"I worry about you. I always have. I will send word as soon as I may."

***

Geoffrey had been feasting on a pie obtained from a flying pieman who hawked his wares from a broad tray hung from his neck and buttressed against his waist.

"I won it, my lady," he said proudly.

"Gambling?"

"In a way. You toss a coin and if you win, you get the pie for free. I suppose it must work out for them at least half the time. I used my own coin."

"What a silly way to do business."

"Business is all gambling, to my mind."

"And what is in your pie?"

"Meat … mostly."

Flour was expensive, and so the piemakers had to cut corners somehow. The filling of "meat" would make up for the badly-made pastry. She refused Geoffrey's offer to pursue the pieman down the street so that she might also sample his wares.

"I am going to move my interest in street food to a more academic and theoretical approach," she told him. "Let us walk for a while. I don't imagine we are too far from the lodgings and it will do me good to have some exercise."

He walked close to her and his looming presence was the best deterrent possible to any potential molesters, botherers, pickpockets, thieves, scruffs, garrotters and general lowlifes. The noise of the horses' hooves and the clatter of the carriage and coach wheels was deafening, although the tone would change as the road surface swapped from stone to flags to clinker to the crushed rocks of macadam. As they passed a hospital, there was a muffling of the noise, due to the road being covered with wood. It was a small concession to the patients suffering within.

"Geoffrey, what do you think of the new police?"

"I think very little of any police, new or old, my lady."

"What are your grounds for your opinion? You know

that I cannot be satisfied with an offhand statement."

They walked on in silence for a little while. She knew he needed time to think. Eventually he said, "I know that they take bribes. I do not like that. In their position, I should take bribes also, which is why I am not a policeman. I know what I am. But they ought to be better than me, and better than the common man. But they are just rough men dressed up all fancy. They're a lie. And this is not the English way."

"Yes, it is obvious to me when they have been paid to look away, or they act only to serve their own ends. I read it daily in the press."

"Just so, my lady. They are involved even now in all manner of crime, exactly as they were back when they were the Runners and would work for whoever paid them the most. And their empire expands and expands, without check."

She didn't reply. She lapsed into thought as they went on. As they passed an opened hatch of a pastry-cook's shop, she stopped and bought some interesting-looking puddings. Geoffrey helped himself to yesterday's stale pastry at half-price. Further on, she was able to buy some bread that had unfamiliar seeds dotted on its crust.

The food was bundled up and Geoffrey carried it back to the lodgings. She was pleased to find Mrs Unsworth was absent, and so she set about the kitchen, trying to bend the small enclosed range to her will. Ruby had been quite correct; few people cooked at home, certainly in the centre of the city. At Clarfields, they still had a large open range, but this new building housed the newer, smaller, 'Kitchener' types and its flues and workings were a mystery to Cordelia. The range had been lit that morning, and was slowly giving off a very low heat, and she applied herself to a new task: the best way to bake biscuits. She felt frustrated that she could not go out and act on her own. She was dependent on everyone else who was abroad, working on her behalf. She felt a little like a spider at the centre of a web.

So to distract herself from her feelings of helplessness, she concentrated on cooking and bakery, and littered half the small kitchen table with her dough-marked notes while she waited for her staff to come back to her with information.

CHAPTER ELEVEN

Mrs Unsworth reappeared when Cordelia was about to tackle her mountain of clearing and washing and cleaning. She did not want to leave the cook to tidy up on her own, especially with Ruby and Stanley engaged elsewhere, but Mrs Unsworth sullenly shooed her mistress from the room. She appeared resentful and angry at the sheer amount of work she now had to deal with, but she was even more resentful and angry at the thought of Cordelia undertaking such lowly tasks herself. She was also convinced that Cordelia would not understand the proper methods of washing up, and when to use the teak sink and when to use the stone one, and so on.

Really, servants are such a funny bunch, Cordelia thought. *But it's not in their nature, really. I suppose they are just people first and servants second. We have made them so.*

Cordelia changed into a day dress, struggling with some

of her articles of clothing alone. She chose a lilac one which showed a fashionable expanse of shoulder; it didn't favour her wide stature but she had brought the most up-to-date clothing she could, to show her at her best in society. Just as she was about to settle down with a book, a note arrived, carried by a boy who waited around in case there was a reply and the potential for more money.

He was right to wait; the note was from Ivy, the wife of the magistrate that Cordelia had met at Gibbs' soiree. She was inviting Cordelia out to afternoon tea. Cordelia dashed off a reply and had to head back to her bedroom to change her clothing once again, to something more suitable to be seen in public.

A little over an hour later, she was sitting at a private table in a lovely, floral-themed tea room in a rather exclusive area of Knightsbridge. Ivy was as warm and welcoming as she had been when Cordelia had last met her.

They talked of polite matters at first. Ivy asked about her column and what she was doing in London. In return, Cordelia asked about Ivy and also her husband. "I believe he is a magistrate," she said, wondering if there might be some value in knowing him.

"He is," Ivy said proudly, "*and* he studied law!"

"Is that unusual?"

"It is less unusual these days," Ivy confessed. "Of

course, the whole landscape of justice is changing as our world changes; did we not speak of progress before? He was a barrister and now he is a serjeant-at-law, which they are trying to do away with, and perhaps this is a less positive aspect of progress, you know, when they throw away good things just because they are old things."

"I'm sorry, he's a what? Serjeant-at-law? What exactly are his duties?"

"Oh, there are not many of his status left now, you know. He is very busy as a sitting magistrate at the Bow Street police courts because they can oversee any crime, not just those committed in their own division, like the other police courts and divisions, who are rather more constrained."

"So the divisions are generally rather self-contained?"

"They are." Ivy was relishing her role as an imparter of information. "Here, have you a pencil? I shall ask the man there for some paper."

"No need, do not trouble the waiter. I always carry a notebook. But why?"

"See here." And Ivy began to sketch out a rough map of London, the Thames cutting it in half from east to west. "The boundaries have changed in the past decade as the police have expanded throughout the metropolitan area — everywhere, indeed, but that magical square in the centre, the City, who cleave to their own police quite outside the system that Peel has introduced everywhere else. I can't imagine that can be allowed to continue, of course."

"So what division is Bow Street in?"

"Presently it is F. And within it there are subdivisions, and then sections, with their section houses or station houses, and then the beats which each policeman must walk. The sergeants run the sections, the inspectors run the subdivisions, and there is a superintendent over all the division."

"So Inspector Hood is but a small cog in his world," Cordelia mused. "That is good to know."

"Hood? Of Bow Street?" Ivy shuddered.

"You know him?"

"I know them all, more or less, by reputation or by sight. My Anthony talks often of his work."

"And what is your husband's opinion of this man?"

"I fear he finds them all a little lacking, to be honest, although of course, my Anthony is far above them and so their paths will naturally have an edge of some conflict," Ivy rambled. "If you know what I mean. Anyway, the magistrate's men are not part of the common herd. Nor are the detectives."

Cordelia understood, once she'd unravelled Ivy's sentence a few times. "Have you heard of Clancey's lodging house?" she asked.

Ivy smiled. "A lodging house? A lower sort? No, I am afraid that such places are unknown to me. But why on earth do you ask all this, of Hood and lodgings and the police?"

Cordelia hesitated. She felt that the fewer people who knew of her investigations, the better; someone out there was a murderer, and word would soon spread. She did not want them to be forewarned.

And yet Ivy was so simple and natural that she found herself confessing all. She kept her voice low and looked around frequently in case someone was lingering behind an aspidistra, eavesdropping on their secrets.

"Do you know roughly where this lodging house is?" Ivy asked, her eyes wide as Cordelia finished her tale.

"Just south of Holborn Road."

Ivy tapped at her hand-drawn map. "I would guess, then, that it is here in F Division. You said she was in the Bow Street cells? That would make sense. Yes, my Anthony is at constant loggerheads with Hood and his ilk."

"I am doomed to come up against unhelpful policemen."

"No," Ivy said. "He is no policeman, remember. And you are in luck for the superintendent there is an honest man, Townsend or Townley or Townhouse or something."

"Indeed? Until this point I'd been led to believe there is not an upstanding man among them."

"No, that is not true, though it suits the public to talk so, of course. No, you may be assured that there are as many honest policemen as there are crooks in the ranks."

"I must thank you most profoundly, Ivy," Cordelia said. Now, after all they had shared, it was inevitable they were on first name terms. "You have been a most erudite and informative companion."

"You are most welcome. The pleasure is all mine."

"Time runs on; I need to be home to see if my servants have discovered anything useful. But before I take my leave, may I ask, do you know anything of politics?"

"You mean to ask, do I know of this Bonneville's friends or enemies? I have to confess that I do not," Ivy said. "My head is filled with my Anthony's work but that is all I have space for in my poor brain, and some would say that it is too much and I am in danger of overheating but, of course, if I stuck only to needlework I fear I'd overheat even more! But please, you must continue with your investigations and also do keep me informed for now I feel most wedded to the outcome. Why, that poor man and his wife, the girl's parents, they must be quite frantic!"

"And so is the girl herself. Yes, Ivy, I shall keep you informed."

Cordelia wrote everything down as soon as she got back to the lodgings, and pinned up Ivy's map to the wall.

CHAPTER TWELVE

By the time that Ruby appeared, late that evening, one wall of the lodging's sitting room was completely covered by cuttings, maps, prints and scribbled notes. Stanley accompanied Ruby, and scurried ahead to the kitchen. Cordelia had lost track of time, and only realised that she was hungry when she caught a whiff of something baked, lingering about Ruby's person.

"Remove your shawl," she said to her maid.

"It is cold, my lady." Ruby tugged at the tasselled woollen garment, tucking her arms and hands out of sight.

"It is not cold. You're hiding a potato, aren't you?"

Ruby glowered but she let go of one corner of her shawl to reveal that she was, indeed, smuggling a potato. Two potatoes, in fact.

"Who is the other for?"

"Stanley."

Goodness, thought Cordelia. *An act of kindness from the maid to the boy. Well, well.* "What on earth has happened today that you feel compelled to thank him?"

"I'm not thanking him," Ruby said airily. "I'm just keeping him from starvation, as I would a dog."

Ruby tossed her head back and went into the kitchen. Cordelia dearly wanted to call her back and insist that she sample some of the potato but that would be a step too far, she felt. If someone stooped to taking food *from* their servants, something was very wrong.

So she huffed to herself and resolved to wait ten minutes before asking Ruby if she were finished.

But after only five minutes, Ruby popped her head back through the door. "Excuse me my lady. Mrs Unsworth here is half-drunk, the shameful sot, but says you have not yet eaten. So would you like…"

Cordelia was in the kitchen as fast as a runaway horse. Ruby smiled as she carved up the two potatoes between three plates, adding some pie, and cheese, and an apple. She laid out a white cloth for Cordelia; it was customary when the mistress entered the kitchen, and even on holiday here in London, certain protocols had to be followed.

Not the one about her cook being sober, however. "Mrs Unsworth has retired to nurse her gin bottle. She should have prepared food for you."

"I did not ask," Cordelia said.

"That is no excuse." Ruby stacked Cordelia's food onto a tray, added various knives and forks and small jars of pickle and chutney, a folded linen napkin in a silver holder, two glasses — one for water and one for sherry — and carried it back into the sitting room, which was having to do double-duty as the dining room. Within a few minutes she had prepared the table almost to the standard that Neville Fry would approve of, and left Cordelia alone to dine while she and Stanley ate from the kitchen table.

Cordelia felt torn between wanting company, wanting to maintain standards, and being pleased that she had time to continue thinking. Still, she called Ruby back through to the main room once she had finished her makeshift meal. "Is Mr Fry anywhere to be found?"

"I will send Stanley out to find him."

The lodgings were cramped and the servants seemed to find it more awkward to share with Cordelia than she did to share with them. Geoffrey and Mr Fry had found various local hostelries appropriate to their stations, and Stanley was able to find the butler quickly. Mr Fry came back and began to clear up, muttering to himself, while Stanley helped, and Ruby came through to the sitting room to tell Cordelia what she had discovered.

"Now, my lady, it was easy enough to find this Albert

Socks' house. And he has far too many servants, all of whom are on the make."

"Excuse me?"

"They skim off from the food and the drink; they abuse his trust and use their positions. And not one of them would I call honest, and all of them are too free with their tongues." Ruby sniffed and looked most supercilious. "They are servants of very low breeding, my lady. But then, I suppose he is only a politician."

"Indeed. And what of Florence?"

"There was a maid who was bringing drink from a nearby alehouse and we talked," Ruby said. "She knew Florence very well. She was definitely being kept by the Lord Brookfield. He had taken her on as a maid in his house but soon her charms persuaded him of other duties that she could perform. Then she was passed to Socks, like a horse being lent out to another."

"And she stayed in Socks' house also? Usually these women are installed in some lodgings of their own."

"The finer ladies are ... I think that would have been the eventual result, perhaps, if she learned to act the courtesan, but for the moment Socks had said to the world that she was another servant, and he expected her to behave as one. In truth, my lady, I do not think this Florence is of high enough character to be a well-liked mistress of a man.

You met her. What do you think?"

"I would agree," Cordelia said. The mistresses of important men who were given rooms of their own were well-spoken, fashionable and often clever women. Florence appeared to be none of those things, although Cordelia had admittedly not met the girl in the best of circumstances. Some lower-bred women were consummate actresses, and learned to show the world an artificial face, but most did not. It took more than changing one's accent; one had to exist as another person entirely. It was difficult.

Ruby got up and paced the room. It was tastefully decorated in deep shades of burgundy, with the woodwork — dado rail, picture rail, frames and windows — picked out in a rich yellow. She wandered to the wall where Cordelia had assembled her information and inspiration.

"But I found out some other interesting things, and there is one other thing which ... you will not be happy about," Ruby said, looking at the wall rather than her mistress.

"What?"

"Let me tell you in order. Firstly, that Albert Socks, and that dead man Bonneville, hated one another."

"They were on the same side."

"Quite so, but it is not unusual in politics, is it? Furthermore, Bonneville and the Lord Brookfield were friends, or at least, they were not enemies."

Cordelia rose to stand next to Ruby. "There is something fishy here, and it is not eels. Have you some ribbon?" She looked at a scrap of paper which said "Socks", and an article which had a print of Lord Brookfield, and the obituary of Bonneville.

With Ruby's help, Cordelia tacked the strips of red ribbon on the wall, making a triangle between Socks, Bonneville and Brookfield.

In the centre she pinned Florence's name.

"I wonder," Cordelia said, "if this girl is more significant than we had been assuming."

"What, some lowly woman like her?" Ruby said, mockingly. "No, surely it is simply a case of her being in the wrong place at the wrong time."

"Yes, but look," Cordelia said, tapping the points of the triangle. "She was Socks' woman but she was in love with his enemy, Bonneville. Was it just a plot by Bonneville to undermine Socks? And if Socks found out…"

"Then he would be even more angry to discover she was using the room that *he* had given her, to meet with his enemy. Then Socks is a suspect, my lady."

"He is indeed."

"Now I have a question for you, my lady," Ruby said. "How was it possible for those two, Florence and

Bonneville, to actually meet? He was not likely to be a guest at Socks' house, so how would a lowly fallen woman meet a politician?"

"That is a good point. Perhaps they met at the Lord Brookfield's house, while she was there, as those two men are friends."

"But they are of such different statuses," Ruby argued. "I struggle to see how their paths would meet. Maybe the Lord Brookfield passed her to him?"

"Or even Socks did."

"No," Ruby argued. "That would make no sense. Why would he pass his woman to his enemy?"

"Perhaps she was not a nice gift," Cordelia said. "I have often wanted to parcel up some fish and send it by slow mail to my distant cousin Hettie."

"I see no problem with that, as long as you do not attach a return address." Ruby took a deep breath. "And now, my lady, I have but one more thing to tell you. You will not like this. Please, sit down."

"Oh, come now, Ruby. What could be so awful?" Cordelia laughed as she obeyed her servant and sat on a wooden chair, fluffing her skirts up as she did so.

Ruby looked reluctant to speak. She blurted it out in a rush. "Hugo Hawke is in town, my lady."

Cordelia was glad now that she had sat down. She

pursed her lips. "And you saw him with your own eyes?"

"From afar, my lady, across the street as we returned back here."

"And did Stanley see him also?"

"No, my lady."

"And the street was crowded, I assume?"

"Well, yes…"

"Then let us be plain, Ruby. You could have seen anyone. Why, one would barely recognise one's own mother if she were on the other side of the street."

"I'd barely recognise her if she were stood here in front of me," Ruby muttered under her breath.

Hugo Hawke was not someone that Cordelia was prepared to worry about. She dismissed him from her mind. "Ruby, I shall retire for the evening."

"Yes, of course, my lady."

106

CHAPTER THIRTEEN

Cordelia had had enough of waiting for other people to do the investigating on her behalf. Ruby and Stanley had had a late night, so she let them sleep in, and she didn't want to explore the local alehouses and dining rooms to find Geoffrey or Neville Fry. She threw a thin, light plain cloak around her shoulders, pilfered from Ruby's chest. Ruby was shorter than Cordelia and it did not reach her ankles. With an unremarkable hat tied under her chin with a dark ribbon, and a basket on her arm, Cordelia decided that in the great big city of London, she could pass as a mere middling sort of merchant's wife, and so move around unmolested. She hoped.

And off she went, striding with a determined air back to the Bow Street station house. She stamped up the steps and into the lobby. There was an unfamiliar policeman in the outer area but she stream-rolled herself over him, using the information and names she had gathered from talking with Ivy Delaney.

"I am here to talk to one of the detectives," she informed the man in uniform.

"And you are…?"

"I just told you, man. I am here to speak to one of the detectives. Do I wait here, or shall you show me to a room? Thank you."

"Are any of them expecting you? Is there one in particular that you want to see?"

"They are not expecting me yet, but I have information that they need." She glared at him. "Any of them will do."

"I don't think—"

"No. You do not think. Which is why you are a mere constable. I do not think I shall be recommending promotion for you to the superintendent, you know. I am Cordelia, Lady Cornbrook. You will have no idea as to the stretch of my influence." *Mostly because it does not stretch very far,* she thought.

"The superintendent?"

She glared even more.

"Very well. Wait here, madam."

He backed away, watching her, and disappeared into a small room. The door closed but swung itself open again, very slightly, leaving a crack due to the warping of the wood.

She moved towards it. An odour of pipe tobacco wafted out.

"Some woman is out there," she heard the policeman say, "reckons on as she is a lady but she looks nothing like, to my mind. Asking for to speak to the detectives, as in, you two sirs, she don't mind which."

"What does she want to talk about?" another voice said.

"I ain't got a clue. The price of bonnets and lace, maybe."

"Oh, send in her. There's precious little else happening so we may as well have some sport."

As the policeman came out of the room, she was already at the door, and she swept past him before he could speak.

The two detectives wore normal clothes. She had discussed this strange phenomenon with Ivy; there was a great deal of bad feeling amongst the public for a man in authority being disguised as a 'normal' person. Who could you trust if they were there, in the crowd, listening? It unsettled people. And yet, Cordelia could see Ivy's argument that it was necessary to help to fight crime. "Criminals must be prevented from committing their atrocities, not simply caught and punished after the fact," Ivy had said. "And to prevent those things, it is necessary for the policeman to move in the same circles as the criminal."

The two men were dressed in sober and unremarkable ways. Both of them got to their feet and performed small, jerky bows before one of them pulled out a chair and offered her a seat.

She introduced herself. They raised their eyebrows and she knew, immediately, that they didn't believe that she was who she said she was. Her 'middling merchant' dress did not match her name and professed rank. How could she prove it? She could not. She forged ahead, anyway.

"I am here on the matter of the murder of Louis Bonneville," she informed them.

Both men were now sitting again. One swung back on his chair, impudently. "We have the culprit in our cells," he said. "What is that to you? Oh … John, do you remember what Hood was saying about that pestilent woman who forced her way into here, with that clergyman who is always buzzing around like a fly?"

"I do, indeed. She claimed to be a lady then, too." He curled his lip, making the sandy edges of his moustaches bristle outwards like a cat that had been startled. He stared at each part of her body in slow succession. She wanted to throw something at him.

"I do not *claim*. I *am*."

"Quite so," the moustachioed-man, John, said blandly. "I am sure that you are. Oh, go on, then. So what frightfully important news do you have for us?"

"You have the wrong person in your cells."

Both of them burst out laughing. "We have the woman who was caught red-handed, right there, in his bed! There was an empty bottle of wine with traces of poison within, a general scene of disarray, and who was she? Some loose woman that is passed from man to man! She does not even charge for it," the man said, slapping his thigh with the sheer hilarity of the whole situation. "Frank, Frank, do you hear? We have the wrong one! Oh, what a day this is. Go on, then. So who ought we to have there in her stead?"

"I am not entirely sure yet," Cordelia said stiffly. "But the suspects that you should look to would start with Mr Albert Socks. Have you spoken with the Lord Brookfield? And the enemies of Bonneville?"

"There is none so vindictive and likely to seek revenge as a woman," one man said. "In fact, your actions in coming here raise *my* suspicions. An accomplice, are you? Some manner of accessory? Oh, that would explain your presence..."

"No!" she said. "Why would you think that?"

"We are men chosen for this role because we think what others do not," the second, Frank, said. "We look for

111

patterns and where the pattern breaks down, there is the crime! And you, madam, are outside of the usual pattern."

"So you see that we must arrest you," the first man said.

Cordelia shot to her feet and clutched the basket in front of her, wishing that she had more hatpins in her hat. But what could she do against two men, in the middle of a station house full of similar men?

She stood, as straight and tall as she could, and weighed up the distance to the door behind her. She would have to turn, and would lose vital seconds in her flight...

Frank and John laughed even harder. "Oh, your face!"

"Ha! She does believe it, Frank, she does! She thinks that we will arrest her!"

"Perhaps, then, there is some guilt in her?"

"Perhaps, indeed! Ha! Ha!"

They were mocking her. She narrowed her eyes but no clever retort came to her. Feeling hot, sweaty and deeply humiliated, she whirled around and stormed out of the room. She pushed past a policeman who was standing in the lobby, elbowing him aside with a quite unnecessary jab to his waist.

She had clear vision. She would *not* let her eyes brim with tears, and nor would she make any kind of scene. She would not stoop to display all those weaknesses that she knew they expected to see in her.

She heard a cry behind her, a small boy's voice, and instinct made her turn her head back even as she pushed through the heavy wooden exit doors. The cry was cut off, and a door slammed somewhere.

It was nothing to do with her. She was moving forward through the door without looking where she was going, and she slammed with great force into a broad-shouldered man who was coming into the police station house.

"Madam," he said, gripping both of her elbows to steady her.

She was glad that she had the basket jutting between them. She saw his face, and she pushed the basket hard into his solar plexus, breaking his hold on her arms.

"Hugo Hawke! You unhand me this *instant*."

CHAPTER FOURTEEN

"Lady Cornbrook!" Hugo Hawke sounded as surprised as she was. Her old nemesis took a step back, and stared.

He had not changed since she had last seen him, the previous summer, when she had been a guest at his Cambridgeshire estate. She had rejected his proposal of marriage, and won her own house from him. As the trustee to her late husband's will, he could have sold Clarfields and left her homeless.

But she had fought him, and she had been triumphant, and she had snubbed him publically, and such things did not sit well with the otherwise jovial and rather good-looking man. He was of the hunting, shooting, fishing set and intended to drink and party his way through life. Cordelia had been the first thing in his life that had not gone his way.

But other things must be going awry now, she thought. "Why are you here, at a police station house?"

"Oh, and it is delightful to see you, too," he said sarcastically. "And I could ask you the same thing."

"You could ask. I would not answer."

"You are the rudest woman I have ever met."

"And you are—"

The door behind Cordelia opened suddenly and caught up in her dresses. The policeman stammered out some apologies and then realised he had walked into an argument. He held the door open as more curious onlookers came out to watch the fuss.

"And you are a cad and a snake, and I assume you are here to hand yourself in for something," Cordelia said haughtily.

"You have no call to say such things, a cheater such as yourself! I thought time might have mellowed you, but you are still a harridan and a—"

"How dare you!" she spat.

Hugo's face was darkening and his fists clenched when something beige and soft hit the side of his head and rebounded to tumble back down the steps. He turned with a cry to face the new onslaught.

Geoffrey was standing at the bottom of the steps, at the head of an amused crowd. He began to walk up the steps towards them. "My lady!" he called stridently. "Have no fear. I am armed."

Hugo put his hand up to his face and wiped at his cheek, then sniffed his hand. "With a pie? You threw a *pie* at me?"

The said object had rolled down the steps and been scooped up into the hands of a passing urchin who ate it hastily.

"I wouldn't waste a real weapon on you," Geoffrey said as he reached out his hand to Cordelia and placed his bulk between her and Hugo. He led her back down the steps.

Hugo shook his fist after them, but then realised that the police were now crowding in from behind. He looked startled, and hurried down the steps, but at an angle so that he came out onto the street about ten feet away from Cordelia and Geoffrey.

"I have powerful friends!" Hugo yelled as Geoffrey lunged into the road and began to wave at passing cabs. "With rather more clout than a coachman and a pie!"

They ignored him. "I was rather enjoying that pie, too," was Geoffrey's only comment as he helped her into a small cab that he flagged down by standing in front of the horse and growling. It was a single-horse fly and left her upper body exposed. She nestled back into the murky-smelling depths. Geoffrey slammed the half-door closed in front of her knees, before climbing up to sit next to the cab's driver at the back, whether the driver wanted him there or not. There was not enough room. Geoffrey sat there anyway.

***

Around two streets from the lodging house, Cordelia banged sharply on the roof of the cab until they stopped. "I fancy walking the final way, to clear my head," she explained as she paid the now-quivering driver. He was keen to be away and she had barely pressed an extra coin into his hands before he had slapped the reins on the horse's back and cried "On!"

"What on earth did you say to him?" she asked Geoffrey. "I heard you talking but I could not make out the words."

"I am a coachman, my lady. I offered him some helpful hints as to his handling and driving."

"Oh dear. Well, thank you for rescuing me from that dreadful Hawke."

"I wish I'd had more than one pie to throw at him, that's all."

She smiled. It had been strange to see the man; once she'd even thought of marrying him. He was good company but their disagreement had soured things irreversibly between them. And she had seen the worst of him, and hadn't liked it.

She supposed that he had also seen the worst of her, too.

She scuffed her feet along the walkway that had been separated from the main part of the road by bollards, in a local experiment to try to cut down on the cases of pedestrians stumbling into horses, and vice versa. "Oh, Geoffrey, I don't think I've really thanked you enough for being so loyal to me over the years."

He grunted and increased his pace, immediately unwilling to engage in any potentially emotional conversation.

"Since *he* ... Maxwell ... died in that awful way, you have stuck with me. In fact, even before, when he was ... acting as he acted ... you were there, protecting me, and you need to know that I am grateful."

He half-shrugged. "My lady, it's my job."

"Don't belittle it like that. You go beyond your job and your role. You know what is right and what is wrong, and you act accordingly." *It might not be right or wrong according to society, but that is another matter,* she thought. "I still think about that night, you know. When he died. My lord husband. I knew he was in no fit state to drive his carriage but I could never tell him so ... and anyway, I wanted him out of the house, away from me. When he was so drunk, it was better that he was nowhere near me, or any person. So perhaps I am to blame. I didn't stop him. I encouraged him. Maybe I even…"

"My lady!" Geoffrey said sharply. "It was an accident and nothing more. You must not talk this way. It was none of your doing and you have no cause to feel guilt, none at all."

She found his paternal care comforting. "And once again you rescue me," she said.

He chose to ignore her meaning — that he had rescued her from herself and her negative emotions — and instead he said, "From Hawke or from the police?" He barked out a laugh though she couldn't see what was funny.

"Of all the places that I ought to feel safe, surely a police station house is one of the best," she said, ruefully, as they reached the lodgings and she drew out her key.

"On the contrary," Geoffrey replied. "Where else will you find such a collection of crime and criminals and ne'er-do-wells?"

"You don't mean down in the cells, either, do you?"

"I do not."

They entered the place which had already become her sanctuary, and she began to relax.

Chapter Fifteen

Two days later, and Cordelia found herself once again abandoning a horrific mess in the kitchen so that she could get ready to go out.

"Not one of these doughs held a good shape after being baked," she complained. She tried to wipe down a floury surface but she used a wet cloth and Mrs Unsworth snatched it from her hands.

"My lady, no! You will make twice as much work for me. Go, go now. I shall see to this. Without help, as well. Alone, mark you, all my girls back at Clarfields…"

"Thank you."

She heard a stifled curse aimed in her direction as she left the kitchen but she decided not to turn and challenge Mrs Unsworth on it. Anyway, the cook had a point. She was the mistress of her own domain and Cordelia was only admitted on sufferance. And Mrs Unsworth usually had a bevy of pale young women to do the rougher work.

Cordelia called Ruby to help her to prepare for the evening's entertainment.

For Septimus Gibbs had been successful on her behalf. She was to be a guest at a ball that night, and he assured her that the Lord Brookfield would also be there.

"And more friends besides," Gibbs said as he led her into the grand assembly rooms just three hours later. "For look, there is Mr Delaney and his wife Ivy."

She scanned the room. It had been decked out with a peach-and-pink theme, and there were great tumbling displays of flowers that were artfully made to seem as if they were in a rococo jungle. The pillars and the pots, all covered in trailing tendrils and cascading flowers, made the large space more intimate as it was divided into nooks and crannies. She caught a few more familiar faces, and most of them were welcome ones. But not all. Her stomach clenched when she caught sight of Hugo Hawke. It was only to be expected that he would be present, but she was glad that he was in animated conversation with a highly decorated army-type man with a curious headdress, and he had not seen her.

"Might you introduce me to the Lord Brookfield?" she said to Gibbs.

"I shall do my very best, dear Cordelia. But he is most

lofty, and I have to work for a living, you know."

"But you yourself are the son of a nobleman!"

"The seventh, alas. They had quite run out of titles and positions by the time my mother had me. I suppose nobody expected that we *all* should live and reach adulthood."

"How … interesting," she said, as she realised that "how unfortunate" and "how fortunate" were both equally inappropriate comments.

"Ah, we might have a chance with the Lord B himself," Gibbs said suddenly, and surged forward with Cordelia on his arm. "He is momentarily alone. If we can catch his eye, then … ah, yes."

Lord Brookfield was a tall and elegant man, with good breeding oozing from every pore, along with the odour of cologne and very aged wine. They went through the typical ritual of greeting. Cordelia knew that she had a limited amount of time to engage him in conversation; courtesy would dictate that they conversed for a while, but also meant that after a minimum period, he would be free to go and speak to his closer friends, and she would have to let him go. Propriety worked both ways. You knew you had an exit and people would be too polite to hold you back.

And it was generally felt that it was crass to speak of politics, women or religion in general conversation. It didn't stop the gossips, but Cordelia didn't want to start out being seen in the wrong light.

Luckily, Lord Brookfield opened up the conversation first. As if reading from a manual of etiquette, he smiled and said, "What a charming bloom you have about your cheeks, my dear. You attend with the esteemed and respectable Mr Gibbs ... forgive me, as I am not up to date with many things. Lord Cornbrook ... I do not know of him. Does he travel abroad?"

"Mr Gibbs is ever my protector and chaperone, and has long been a friend to my family. Sadly my Lord Cornbrook passed away a few years ago and I have been re-entering the world by slow degrees. He is ... was not of your station and did not move in London circles."

"Please accept my condolences, and also my shame that I did not know."

Why would he know? Though the exalted ranks of the aristocracy were small and insular, the country families like the Cornbrooks were scattered and varied. There was spreading nobility and titled persons of lesser rank everywhere, two-a-penny at every Hunt Ball and County Show.

"Indeed," he went on, "you and I have something in common, for I too lost my very dear spouse, the incomparable Rebecca, although many years past now. We have been blessed with a daughter who is married and has, herself, been blessed in her turn by many children of her own. I keep a small house, now, but it is periodically invaded by those laughing terrors." He chuckled amiably. "I am lucky. I get to enjoy their youth and frivolity, and I also get to hand them back as I tire of them, and reclaim my sanctuary once more."

"Sadly I have not been in such a privileged position," she said, and he immediately changed the subject so as not to cause her distress.

"Do you commonly reside in London?"

"I am visiting," she said. "I have taken lodgings quite centrally, and I intend to soak up as much culture and high-minded pursuits as I can."

"Ah, the museums, the galleries. Quite so," he said. "Our grand heritage makes us a great nation and our empire is slowly amassing the fortunes and the treasure of the whole world and bringing them back here for all to delight in."

He said it as if the theft of another country's treasure was a good thing, and from the look on his face, he truly believed it. There was a jingoistic jutting of his chin. Before he could launch into a stirring rendition of the national anthem, she said, "As well as art, I am also interested in architecture." It was a blatant lie. She hoped that he would not turn out to be a world-acknowledged expert and engage her in difficult conversation.

"Are you?" he said. "Well, London offers you the very best in such things."

"Yes," she said, ploughing on in spite of his lack of encouragement; clearly he wasn't interested, or he'd still be asking questions. "One place I intend to visit would be the Houses of Parliament."

"Do you not mean the Palace of Westminster?" he said.

"Ah … yes, I probably do. I should say that though I am interested in architecture, I'm not an expert…"

"It is still, alas, something of a building site, a rather rough work in progress," he said sadly. "The dreadful fire in thirty-four took much of the more ancient fabric of the building. Still, now that Barry and Pugin have their teeth into it, I am sure we might see a new and even more majestic edifice arise."

"And does work — political work, I mean — still go on while it is rebuilt?"

"It does, of course. I am a member of the House of Lords, and we are determined to ensure that the country will be run as it ought to be, regardless of what surrounds us."

"Indeed, and I commend you." She drew in a breath as she prepared to break social convention. Her whole

126

conversation had been designed to lead subtly to this point, to make it look as casual and innocent as possible. If she'd brought up politics right at the start, without preamble, she would have seemed rude. "I would fancy that all politicians, of whatever shade they might be, have but one aim deep in their hearts: that of the advancement of the welfare and rights of our people."

"Welfare, certainly, but I would disagree about rights. For it is a plain fact, my lady, that the common man does not really know what is best for him. Such knowledge is given to us, to the few in power, so that we might guide and lead while absolving the lesser mortal of the responsibility to make decisions about which he is not capable, due to lack of education, or breeding, or simply common sense. Not all have the aptitude to think great things, do they?"

"Indeed they do not," she said, agreeing while still feeling uncomfortable about his argument. She wasn't sure why it unsettled her, but it did. Still, Lord Brookfield was only saying something that was common knowledge to everyone. "And do all politicians naturally have this aptitude, or are some there by accident of birth?"

He allowed a brief look of shock to tweak his eyebrows. He cleared his throat before he said, carefully, "Goodness, that was unexpectedly bold, my lady."

"It is probably my lack of husband that makes me so free with my tongue."

"Ah, the widow's prerogative."

"It is that. Indulge me. I have rather taken an interest in politics since coming here."

"It would be a most unseemly interest."

"Well," she hurriedly countered, thinking on the fly as fast as she could, "of course, not the tedious subject of politics itself. No, no. I do confine myself to the more fitting considerations regarding, um, the nature of man and what values, what, er, exalted values a man would have who entered politics, and ... and, well, just what I said." She stumbled out of rhetoric and into gibbering. "I shall ignore the minute substance and detail of a man's beliefs; but do all politicians in general hold heartfelt beliefs, or do they wax and wane according to what befits their ambition?"

He was growing tired, and not a little uncomfortable with the conversation. He smiled thinly, and said, "As to that, I do not claim to hold any insight into a man's private motivations."

She noticed he was no longer asking her questions, as he did not wish to prolong the conversation.

"Indeed not, and you must forgive my impertinence," she said.

"The widow's prerogative again?"

"Some might say I was impertinent all my life," she said, and he smiled a little more naturally.

But she still hadn't managed to steer the conversation onto the main topic she needed. She could see the moment passing. In desperation, as he relaxed once more, she blurted out, "For example, I am curious about one Albert Socks. A politician in your own party, is he not?"

Lord Brookfield went absolutely still and she realised her mistake instantly. Oh, to turn back time! She should have mentioned one or two other men, first, and Socks would then be an incidental name in a list of names. By speaking his name first, she had made him the main event, and aroused suspicion.

I am not as clever as I think I am, she berated herself. *It is too late to turn this around. I shall watch him closely, however, as I still might learn something.*

Lord Brookfield smiled again, and it was a distant and patronising one. "My dear lady Cornbrook, Mr Socks is but one member of a very large party of diligent and hard-working men, all with but one aim in mind: the betterment of the nation. We might all disagree on the methods by which we'll achieve this, but no matter. As to the individual himself, why, our paths do not cross. Ah! Mr Gibbs. I fear your good lady friend is growing tired of this unfamiliar social whirl."

"Cordelia!" Gibbs was concerned immediately as Lord Brookfield passed her over into his care, and bowed his way backwards, sidling out of sight as quickly as he could. "What ails you?"

"Absolutely nothing," she said, "save that I have taken my already tarnished reputation and added 'foolish prattle' to it."

"Have you asked indelicate questions?"

"I have," she said defiantly.

"Oh dear. Do not let your actions besmirch me, if you please."

"I shall try not to. Perhaps you should not be seen with me," she said, beginning to grin.

"What are you proposing?"

"That you go and fetch me a fresh glass of champagne," she retorted. "And thereby reduce the damage to your reputation by being in my company."

He raised his eyes to the heavens and mouthed a silent prayer, but he was smiling as he took her empty glass and went in search of more drink.

It was unfortunate, then, as she found herself alone at the edge of a small anteroom at the ball, that this was the moment that Hugo Hawke descended upon her, and pulled her into a curtained alcove beside a bust of Cicero on a pillar and a portrait of the late King Edward VII who frowned down upon them as she slapped at Hugo's chest ineffectually.

"What do you mean by this? Let go of me!"

"Hush," he said, and moved his hand as if to press it to her mouth. He stopped short as she grabbed the cravat around his neck and began to twist, strangling him by inches. "Stop," he gasped, and she released the pressure slightly.

"What do you mean by this?" she asked again, and kept her hand firmly ready to choke him again if she did not like his answer.

Chapter Sixteen

"Listen," he said in a rough, low voice. "We are fighting for the same thing."

"I ... what do you know of what I am fighting for?"

"You're investigating that politician's murder, aren't you?" he said.

"What murder?"

"For goodness' sake, Cordelia. Don't play games with me. We've been through too much together."

She didn't like any association of "together" with Hugo Hawke, but she let her hand drop from his neck. He was right. And she was, she had to admit, intrigued. "There might be a private matter to which I am attending, yes. A *private* matter."

He straightened his necktie. "As soon as I heard it involved that old butler of yours, and his daughter, I knew you'd be all over it like fleas on a hedgehog. Not that I knew he had a daughter! The old goat." He chuckled. "Anyway, you are quite the lady-detective now, you know. And when I saw you at the station house, then I knew for sure. And I know something else, too."

"What?" She hated to ask for information, but she wanted to know what mischief he was up to, and then make her escape back to the ball. Conversations and chatter drifted past them, against an aural backdrop of dancing music.

"The police are thwarting you. Aren't they?" he said.

"They are," she had to agree. "What do you know of it, though?"

"I know enough. I know that they will stand in your way, and that the poor girl has just been thrown to the wolves for it."

"And what do you care?"

"I care nothing for her," he said, lightly. "But the police are thwarting me, too, and that — well, I do care about that."

She was taken aback. Now she was leaning in to him, rather than trying to get away. "You must start from the beginning," she said. "You don't even live in London!"

He glanced around, and peeped around the pillar, before pulling the curtain even more tightly closed to shield them from view. "Consider this a kind of truce between us," he said, "And afford me the honour and courtesy of keeping my words private."

"Of course." *Unless a crime is committed,* she added in her head. He could see her hands so she imagined crossing her fingers. That would have to do. And she was so surprised that he was confiding in her at all, that she even wondered if he had changed in some way; had a conversion, perhaps, or a life-changing illness. She listened.

"Well," he said, "I own property, as you know. I must have the rental income, especially since you ... enough of that."

He was referring to Clarfields. She flared her nostrils, and he continued, hastily.

"And one of the properties that I own is a public house, not far from here. I installed a publican who is responsible for the day to day running of the place. He is the one under licence from the local magistrates to sell all alcohols and spirits. Everything is done by the book."

"Indeed."

He glared at her. "Indeed it is. But the local police in that division, Holborn, are trying to blackmail this man, my publican. He runs boxing matches, just small affairs for the common man, nothing out of the ordinary."

Alarm bells began to sound in Cordelia's head. She watched Hugo closely.

He went on. "But the policemen, you see, are insisting that my publican gives them money to be able to continue running these entertainments, or that they will have him up on charges of disorderly conduct and goodness knows what else. They could fabricate anything. Who are they accountable to? Nobody, as far as I can see."

"That all seems suspiciously plausible," she said. "What are you not telling me, Hugo? And if you are having problems with Holborn, why were you at Bow Street?"

His gaze flickered away. He checked the curtain again, running his hands down the thick folds, tugging it into place. "I'm telling you everything," he said. His tone turned wheedling. "Isn't this like old times, Cordelia? Do you remember, you and I, at the start of your visit to my house? What fun that was? Just like old times..."

"Not quite," she said. "I cannot see a handy set of stairs to kick you down."

He winced as he remembered the blow she had fetched him, in front of all of his guests and friends. "Let us not speak of that," he said.

She wondered if the bitterness of that time would still be burning him, deep inside. That was another reason for her to be suspicious of him. "Why are you telling me these things?" she said. "You must be plotting against me, somehow ... you must be! Let me assure you that I shall not be taken in by you again! Not ever, sir."

"I am telling you, Cordelia, you stupid, stubborn thing, because I need your help."

She gaped at him for a moment.

"You look like a trout."

She closed her mouth, and said, "And you claim to need my help? With flattery like that?"

"True flattery never did work on you, so I might as well be honest," he said. "I thought you might respect that. Respect what I am saying, even if you don't respect me. Listen, it is true. We can work together. You will be investigating this murder, and I need to find evidence, hard evidence, that I can bring against the police. I had gone to Bow Street because I thought they could help me against Holborn. They won't; I need evidence of the wrongdoing!"

"To take them before the magistrates?"

"Yes, exactly that. But how can one expose the injustice perpetrated by the justice system itself? What's the saying, who guards the guards? It's something in Latin, I don't know. Look, as a man, I can go places that you cannot, so I can look out for information for you. But you … I need you because you have a strange sort of brain, a womanly one, I should say. You talk to unusual people. Like all of your sex, you look at things from a curious angle. I cannot fathom how you do it, but you do. It is your strength as well as your weakness."

"Then ask any woman," she said. "If, indeed, we all have corkscrew minds."

"Yours is the twistiest I have ever encountered. I mean that in a nice way. You will look at the problem sideways and you will come up with connections that I could not see. All I ask is that as you look into things, look into the police, and pass to me anything that you can discover. I am not even asking you to go to extra effort for me. Just be alert."

"I do not know what to say," she said. She was inclined to take his odd words as a kind of compliment.

"Think on it. I'll be in touch." He reached out as if to shake her hand or press it to his lips, but she turned on a high-grade withering stare and he let his fingers drop.

He slid out of the alcove and she remained behind for a few minutes, thinking. He had not behaved too inappropriately with her. He had kept his distance. Could she believe him? Eventually she peered out from the curtain and when she was certain that no one would remark on her movements, she slipped out and re-entered the throng.

She was immediately drawn into a conversation with a small group of people. One man was being somewhat disparaging about her column, teasing her for her "literary pretensions" and she could not argue back because everyone was laughing as if it were merely a very good joke.

138

She did not want to look cold and churlish. But Ivy appeared, and caught her discomfort, and cleverly turned things to other matters.

When a newcomer then mentioned the matter of Bonneville's murder, Cordelia's ears pricked up once more. "Who were the man's enemies?" she asked, but she received general smiles for her answer.

"That woman who is to hang for it, obviously! Some gin-drinker of the streets."

The consensus was that Florence was likely to be guilty of something, and if it were not murder of this man at this time, then she would probably have killed him in the future anyway.

Cordelia felt herself get quite angry. "It is too neat, too pat that she was there in the room when he was killed; no one has come up with any convincing reason why she might have done it! She has no motive."

"I once dropped my cigar in my brandy," a man said. "I half-knew I was doing it, but I cannot really explain why I did it. A part of me was curious as to the effects. I was, perhaps, distracted and idle."

"And drunk," someone added.

"That is a completely different thing," Cordelia said in shock. "No one kills on a whim, just to see what happens."

A matronly woman stepped in. "*All* of this talk is

unseemly and inappropriate," she said. "We are not in some common coffee house, and this reflects badly on every one of you. Of us. And our host would not approve."

The talk was forcibly turned once more. Cordelia sank into thought.

"And drink," that person had said. It chimed in her head.

Was Florence guilty? Cordelia had to consider the possibility. Could it be a crime of passion?

No, she thought. A crime of passion would be something violent and physical, in the heat of the moment, using whatever came to hand. Bonneville had been poisoned by wine.

That had to be have been planned, Cordelia thought.

And then another thing came to her which turned her thoughts around.

Neville Fry assured her that his daughter did not — indeed, could not — drink alcohol.

If that was common knowledge, and her lover knew and accepted it, then she could easily refuse to drink the poisoned wine without arousing suspicion. If she had poisoned the wine herself, she had a good excuse why she was not drinking it.

Suddenly, it was not looking good in Florence's favour, Cordelia realised. She had to look harder for a motive.

CHAPTER SEVENTEEN

Gibbs accompanied her right back to the door of her lodgings at Furnival's Inn that night. He took her in his own enclosed carriage rather than chancing the chillier cabs that thronged the streets. Still, she insisted on having the carriage window open, and he assumed that she needed the air due to the over-consumption of champagne. But in reality, she was fascinated by the city at night.

"The streets never sleep," she said, as they got stuck behind a succession of cabs and coaches. "I reckon it to be a long way past midnight and yet the place is teeming like a midweek afternoon."

"Teeming with a different character of people, though," Gibbs said, as he nestled back and ignored her entreaties to look outside.

"You imagine they might all be lowlifes and drunkards and women of questionable morals," Cordelia said, "and though there is a share of that sort, in fact I see workers coming home and workers setting out, and all manner of trades about their business. How long until dawn? I suppose there are people who must walk a great distance to be at the markets, to buy their produce, to be able to sell them to others who will be going to walk in a few hours' time." She was reminded once more of her desire to visit Billingsgate, and other places.

They passed a man selling hot cakes and coffee but Gibbs refused to let her ask the driver to stop. "You will not sleep at all tonight," he said, reprovingly. "Do not touch the stuff."

In fact, once he had delivered her to the door, she didn't sleep anyway. Instead, she crept into the lodgings quietly and sat herself at the table in the main room, still in her dancing slippers with her sheer shawl loose about her shoulders and her hair now frizzing and uncurling. By the light of a tall, thick candle with a mirror at its back, as the sky faded from black and orange to grey and paler grey, she read through her notes once more, and then sat back, trying to force her mind to move sideways just as Hugo had said it would.

She was drawing out connections on a large sheet of paper when Ruby appeared at the connecting door to their room. She had a brown woollen shawl pulled around her shoulders and was still in her long nightdress. She blinked blearily. "My lady? Are you well?"

"Ah, Ruby, will you see to a pot of tea please?"

Ruby came forward and snuffed out the half-burned candle. "Have you been up all night, my lady? If so, it's not tea that you need, it's your bed."

Cordelia waved her hand in dismissal of that arrant good sense. "Of course, of course. But listen, Ruby, I have worked out what I need to do next."

"As I said. You need to go to bed."

"In good time. Oh, Stanley, good morning; do come in. Go through."

The youth had to cross the sitting room to get from his sleeping area to the kitchen, due to the cramped layout of the rented rooms. No secret back stairs to hide the servants from the masters here. He dipped his head and scuttled around the edge of the room as Cordelia continued to speak. "No, I need to visit the lodging house where the man died. I must see for myself what manner of place it is, and I must gain entry to the room itself, and examine it."

"What would you hope to discover there?" Ruby asked. Stanley paused by the kitchen door.

"I don't know, which is why I must go. It was an odd place to meet. I am concerned that it was Socks who gave her the use of the room. That raises my suspicions. It is not an ordinary act." Cordelia stretched and stood up. "Is my new cloak ready?"

"It is, my lady."

"Perhaps I can go in disguise, then," Cordelia said.

Ruby put her foot down, literally and figuratively. "Absolutely not, my lady. Every one of us would prevent such foolishness." Stanley, still present, was frantically nodding though he didn't dare to speak.

"But—"

"No, my lady. I know I speak out of turn. But you must see sense. You are not the heroine in a silly gothic novel."

Cordelia sagged as all of a sudden, the sleepless night caught up with her. She put her hands on the back of the chair she'd just vacated and leaned her weight forward. "Oh, it all seems impossible. Many others have disguised themselves. Why, haven't there been women who have run away to sea, or joined the army? Women who have had amazing adventures in spite of their sex?"

"About half a dozen of them, all told, my lady, out of millions and millions."

"Those are the ones we know about. Maybe more of us have chanced it than we will ever know. There are ways to manage it. I could darken my top lip with soot, and speak in a gruffer tone…"

Ruby sighed so heavily that Cordelia stopped talking.

She was just about to wend her way reluctantly to bed when Stanley finally spoke. With his customary stammer, and not looking directly at her, he said, "My lady, may I offer a potential solution?"

"Please do," she said, feeling her tiredness ebb away a little.

"Well, it is this. The ladies in the local church which I have begun to attend often visit the deserving poor hereabouts as part of their mission. They can go to some very low places, for of course they are protected by righteousness."

Cordelia glared at Ruby before she could snort in derision.

"Go on, Stanley."

"So you could perhaps accompany them, my lady, on their tours of the slums and the like. You will still be in disguise, in a way."

"Yes," said Ruby, who could disguise her mirth no longer. "You will be disguised as a righteous lady!"

"Ruby! Hold your tongue. The boy's suggestion is sound. It is of some regret to me that I cannot walk as freely as you…"

"I am protected by my poverty," Ruby said.

"…nor, indeed, speak as freely as you," Cordelia added in a warning tone. "Well. I am going to bed for a few hours.

And Stanley, this is an excellent idea. Please see it done. I leave this in your capable hands."

CHAPTER EIGHTEEN

Her night of activity and the resultant sleep through the best hours of the morning, a time when she was usually active, had ruined the full day for her. She was reminded that she was no longer a young woman, and could not take such liberties with her body. She pampered herself, remaining in the rented rooms, eating simple food and lying on the couch.

But the following day, she was ready for action, and it was as well that she was, for Stanley had succeeded.

Somehow he had persuaded the Ladies of East Street Mission that the street which housed Clancey's lodging house was in dire need of some spiritual enlightenment. Stanley took Cordelia to meet them. Cordelia was dressed very simply and plainly, as befitted a humble Christian woman, and before Stanley could introduce her with her real name, she stepped forward and told everyone that she was called Mabel Entwistle.

He could not stammer out a query in time. The four women, a mix of young, old, and exceedingly old, all accepted her immediately and drew her into their throng. Stanley faded away, to wait for her return at the church, while Cordelia found herself in the centre of the group of warm, righteous women as they surged through the streets, fired up from within by their task and their faith.

At first, Cordelia felt a little out of place. Indeed, with the genuine fervour of the ladies surrounding her, she began to experience a twinge of guilt. Cordelia had been raised in the Anglican Church, like almost everyone she knew, and followed the liturgical year with a clockwork monotony borne of habit and familiarity. Over-familiarity, perhaps. She did not have Stanley's deep evangelical passion nor, at the opposite end of things, Geoffrey's shocking atheism. She was occasionally curious about what might "lie beyond" but the day to day questions of people and everyday life occupied her thoughts far more than spiritual matters. And now she was here, pretending to be as moved by the Spirit as the women around her, and she knew she was a liar, and that felt wrong.

But soon she was distracted from her unease as the ladies set about their tasks. They entered a back street, a veritable rookery, and the women walked as confidently as if they had been moving about their own drawing rooms. The ground was filthy and just a mixture of earth, rubble and dark, steaming manure. She hoped it was mostly from horses. There was vegetable matter and rubbish, but not much of that; then she saw a boy with a basket, his bare feet sinking into the morass, as he hunted for that particular pearl beloved of the tanners: dog excrement, or as it was more euphemistically known, "pure."

She turned her face away but one of the ladies, a young woman called Mrs Shirley, did not. She sprang forward with her gloved arms outstretched to entice the boy to her.

Cordelia watched for a while as the woman tried to examine the lad for sores, and persuade him to come to the mission that weekend so that he might be given some shoes. He danced away out of her grasp.

Not one of the women called him ungrateful; they sighed and continued on. They knocked on doors, and spoke to the occupants. They offered food, comfort, and prayers. The food was gladly taken though the rest was merely tolerated.

And finally they came to the street that Cordelia knew the lodging house to be on. Throughout all of this, no one had asked Cordelia any personal questions. Their talk was of their work, and their work only; she began to admire their single-minded purpose and their absolute clarity.

When they received abuse, they bore it stoically. When someone threw a clod of earth and yelled the most vile things, they smiled and wandered on. Cordelia wanted to lag behind and throw a rotten apple back towards the assailant, but she did not. She was Mabel Entwistle, she reminded herself, and modelled her actions and responses on those being demonstrated by the ladies of the mission.

Now Cordelia began to feel tense. The ladies knocked on doors and tried to persuade the occupants to let them in, or at least minister to them on the street. They didn't ask for names, and Cordelia realised she would have no way of knowing which of the lowly-looking buildings would house Mrs Clancey and her lodgers. The houses were in a terraced row, of sooty London brick, and though in many cases the front steps had been scrubbed and the windows cleaned, still there was a sad air of poverty about the place.

Mrs Shirley noticed Cordelia's worried air and came to her side. "Dear Mrs Entwistle," she said, "are you quite well?"

"I am, thank you," Cordelia replied, "but sometimes I do find these streets oppressive."

"Of course, as do we all, though do remember that none of us are alone, for our Saviour walks with us and guides the work that we do here."

"Thank you, yes. I wonder if I might be allowed a

moment or two of peaceful reflection?" Cordelia said.

"You must refill yourself from the wellspring of all life," Mrs Shirley pronounced.

"Er, yes, that's exactly it," Cordelia said.

"We shall proceed to the end of the street and then turn around to come back along the other side," Mrs Shirley said. "Let me procure you a chair and you might sit and pray on the Lord."

"Thank you. That would be much appreciated."

Within moments, Mrs Shirley had begged a hard wooden chair from a house, and installed Cordelia in a quiet spot at the entrance to a dead-end alley that ran between two of the houses, so that she was half-hidden and could meditate in relative privacy.

And then the ladies were away, knocking on the next door and the next. Cordelia leaned forward and peeped around the edge of the brickwork. When they had gone far enough that they were out of earshot, and appeared totally focussed on their work, she called for a boy who was loitering nearby. "Lad, would you like to earn a penny?"

"Mebbe," he said. He had a most unattractive candle of mucus hanging from a nostril, but he dashed it away with a grubby hand, and his eyes were bright. "Penny first, though. What you want, then, missus?"

"I would like to know which house is Mrs Clancey's

lodging house."

He shrugged. "Penny, then. Nah, tuppence."

She pulled out a small coin. "One penny, and that is more than you deserve." *I should have started with a ha'penny and worked up,* she thought. She waved the coin at him. "Tell me, and you shall have it."

After a brief impasse, he indicated a house farther down the street, said, "It's got a blue door and a smell," grabbed the penny and ran away.

She looked down to the house with the blue door.

The ladies of the mission were between her and it.

She sat back and sighed. She would have to wait.

***

She planned what she was going to do as she waited for her chance. The ladies were five houses away from where she sat. The lodging house was seven houses away, on the same side of the street. After the lodging house, there were three more doors until the end of the street where the ladies would turn around and come back up the other side, and they'd have Cordelia in their view the whole time.

So she had a very small sliver of time to get from her hiding place to the house, and inside that house, before the ladies turned.

Her heart began to hammer. She prepared some speeches and explanations in her head as she peered around the corner, watching for her moment. She had to have a reason to give, to explain her presence, if she were caught. "Moved by the Spirit" seemed like the likeliest option but the one that she also found the most distasteful, as it felt somewhat insulting to lie about something that was the bedrock of the ladies' most genuine beliefs.

But I am doing this for the right reasons, she thought, *and if they knew, I am sure they'd understand.*

Could I tell them my true purpose? I could have. It is a little late, now. And anyway, she reminded herself, *they would simply tell me to leave it to the police, I am sure.*

And then, before she could berate herself any longer, the moment arrived and she seized it. The mission ladies had moved on to the house just past the lodging house, after having had the door closed in their faces there. At the next house, the ladies huddled around, and seemed to be engaged in deep conversation with someone at the door there. One or two of them went into the house itself.

Cordelia walked briskly to the blue door of the lodgings. She hurried but did not run. When she reached it, she did note the smell but it was nothing unusual beyond a hint of cooked fish. She tapped, and then tried the handle, and it opened immediately.

She found herself in a very dark, long hallway. Footsteps sounded on a wooden floor up ahead, but no one came to see her and she realised she had knocked too quietly.

She surmised that the rented rooms would be upstairs. Often the landladies of these properties lived on the ground floor and she took the chance that it would be the same here. She crept up the stairs. There was a strip of thin carpet down the centre, and she kept to it, to minimise the sound of her tread.

But she knew that she would have to speak to someone, at some point, and so when she heard hammering as she reached the first floor, she went towards the noise, and found a workmen in rough overalls with a plank of wood across a sawhorse.

"Sorry, missus, am I in your way?" he said. "I'll not be a minute. Hang on."

"Er, no, it's all right," she said. "Please continue. What are you doing?"

He stared at her for a moment, as it was an odd question, but he must have decided that she was an odd woman, and so to be looked upon kindly. He spoke to her gently. "Well, missus, I'm a joiner, you see. That means I work in wood. Actually I should be in a workshop but they have me here as a carpenter because they are cheap and do not want to pay twice."

She had no idea as to the difference, but she smiled and nodded. "And you are repairing the door frames," she said.

"That's right. I do all manner of jobs here, and along this street, from time to time." He seemed to appreciate the break from his task because he stood upright and began to stuff a pipe with tobacco.

Perhaps it was a clue. She seized on it. "My friend often comes here," she said, innocently. "Maybe you've seen her, a pretty young thing, you'll have noticed her, name of Florence, well, Flo to us, of course."

The man shook his head, concentrating on packing the bowl of his pipe. He pushed in firmly with a rough, calloused thumb. "No, missus, not really seen much of anyone if I'm honest. I get on with my work. Most people here come and go and have reason to not be seen, if you gets my meaning. Well, you understand, as you are here yourself. There are more respectable places a body can go."

She quailed a little at the assumption he'd just made about her, then reminded herself that she was in disguise, and so his insinuation was actually a compliment. In a way. She said, "I understand completely. Actually I do not have a room here. Not yet. I was simply looking around. I was wondering about the privacy..."

He raised his eyebrows as he looked up from the pipe and stared at her anew. "Indeed? Well, as private as any other place."

"And the doors lock from the inside?"

"With a key that only the occupant has, generally."

"And different keys to each room?" she asked. "Or could someone in the room next door gain access?"

He laughed. "Different, obviously, otherwise everyone would be robbed and the landlady quite at fault. Sometimes there are multiple copies as some rooms might be let to more than one person for, well, various reasons."

"Of course, that makes perfect sense," she said. Socks would have kept a key and so would Florence; the joiner's words did not contradict anything Florence had told them.

"Look, you seem nice," the man said suddenly. "There is one thing you should know, if privacy and security are so important to you. All the rooms on one floor actually share the same key."

"You said they were different!"

"Yeah, from floor to floor, but it's easier for the landlady to have each floor the same, but everyone gets told they are different, otherwise they would worry, or steal. I know this to be true, because I have worked on the locks."

"So others would know about it, also."

"They shouldn't. But they might. I wouldn't risk it,

here, missus. Not if you need privacy. Try another place for your ... needs."

She dropped her voice. They seemed to be establishing a rapport, now, so she sidled a little closer, and said, "There was a murder here, was there not?"

"Yeah, there was. Oh! Florence, you said. That's the one as did it. Your friend, eh?" He looked at her a little more sternly. "Your friend in truth?"

"She is innocent," Cordelia said. "But I wonder ... can you tell me which room?"

"No, see, it really isn't seemly for..."

He stopped arguing when she passed him a whole florin. His eyes nearly fell out of his head. Two shillings was a decent amount of money. He pocketed it, and pointed at a door at the end of the corridor.

"I assume no one has rented it yet?"

"No, it has not been touched."

But when she pushed the door open, she saw that it had been touched — the place was clean of blood, and the narrow bed was bare, stripped even of its mattress. There was a long-legged table by the head of the bed, and a small square rag-rug on the floor. She could see through the wide woven slats of the bed base that an empty chamberpot nestled under there. There was a stub of a candle on the table, but apart from that, the room was vacant.

157

She crossed to the window and tentatively pulled the thin curtains aside, but immediately saw that the window had been painted shut over many generations. She spun around and sighed. Was this really the room that Albert Socks had rented? Surely he could have afforded better?

She sniffed the air. It smelled clean, in here at least.

There was a tall closet, a wooden cupboard that ran floor to ceiling, on the wall opposite to the bed. It had double doors with mismatching tortoiseshell handles. Again, she was disappointed when she opened it. It was empty. Not even a rail to hang one's clothes upon.

No, she realised suddenly. The room had been cleaned but the wardrobe interior had not. There was white powdery dust on the floor of it, in two little piles.

She touched a gloved finger to it, and sniffed, but there was nothing remarkable about it. It reminded her of plaster dust. She examined the back of the wardrobe more closely. She was no joiner — unlike the man who even now was lingering in the corridor outside — but she could see that someone had been working on the wood panel. Carefully, she tapped, and it rang hollow, as she expected it to.

But it also moved.

She reached up and down, pressing at the edges and corners.

It moved more. It was not fixed at all. She pulled off

her gloves and dug her fingernails into the edges, and the whole panel came forward. She angled it, and peered around one long edge.

She was looking straight into a darkness that was lit by one long slit of light. She reached forwards and pushed past a long velvet jacket until her hand touched warm wood, and she realised she was reaching into the wardrobe of the room next door.

There was no wall between the cupboards.

And only one back, which was removable.

Removable, most easily, from the other room, not this one.

And recently, done, too. Before the murder?

Almost certainly, she thought.

And who did this work? The joiner outside?

"Bill, what are doing? I don't pay you to stand around and smoke your pipe."

The voice was female, but low and gruff. Cordelia leaped out of the wardrobe and into the main room. She was just coming in to the corridor when she saw the joiner, hastily shoving his still-unlit pipe into his pocket. He was going back to his sawhorse, and he called out, "Mrs Clancey! Not at all. I was just telling this prospective tenant here all about the rooms."

Mrs Clancey advanced upon them, and Cordelia found

herself trying to stand taller. Cordelia had height, but Mrs Clancey stood a few inches higher, with wide shoulders and a jutting jaw that was set at a belligerent angle. Her eyes were so pale as to merge into her grey face, and her blonde hair was lank and lifeless. Likely the woman had never smiled in her life, though she doubtless had won a few prize-fights.

"And who are you and how did you get in?"

Cordelia reacted automatically. She said, stiffly, "I am Cordelia, Lady Cornbrook, and I came in through the unlocked front door."

"A lady?" the joiner snorted in disbelief. "And my left foot is the Earl of Bedford."

Mrs Clancey looked down her prominent nose at Cordelia, equally unimpressed. "Well, whoever you claim to be, you can clear out. You have no business here, none at all."

"I was interested in renting a room," Cordelia said, answering as haughtily as she could.

Both the joiner and the landlady laughed, but the landlady's mirth had no humour at all in it. "Get down those stairs or I shall throw you down myself."

Cordelia weighed up her chances in a struggle, and decided to go willingly. She tried to walk down the shabby stairs with dignity but the stairwell was unlit and she had to watch her footing rather than hold her head high and glide down.

When she reached the door to the street she hesitated. She wanted to ensure she wasn't seen leaving the building, although she could probably bring out one of her pre-prepared excuses if the ladies did question her.

Mrs Clancey was not happy that she had paused. She shoved Cordelia hard between the shoulder blades, and said, "Get yourself out of my house this instant, hussy."

Cordelia was not used to being manhandled. She turned and said, "Touch me again and I shall summon the police to you, madam! I am leaving, and let that be enough for you."

But the door opened from the street inwards so she had to pull it towards herself when she turned again, and Mrs Clancey took the chance to push her sharply, sending her tumbling out into the street.

Cordelia stumbled and one knee touched the floor but she jumped up to her feet in an instant, brushing down her dress. The ladies of the mission were ahead of her, but they heard the commotion and turned around to see what was going on. They were surrounding her immediately.

"Mrs Entwistle! What has happened?"

Mrs Clancey still stood in her doorway, filling the frame. "Mrs Entwistle? Aha, you are found out! Lady

Cordelia, Lady Cornbrook, whatever it is you claimed to be. As if! What a stupid thing to say you are. How did you ever expect to be believed? Why, I should say I am the Queen of Sheba!"

It seemed very important to Cordelia that she make everyone understand who she actually was, but she could see that it was impossible. To be misidentified was a strange sort of pain, she thought fleetingly, and felt rather helpless. She was not protected by the knowledge of her status.

She was just a woman on the streets.

She was vulnerable.

Goodness, she thought suddenly, *does Ruby feel like this all the time?*

"What is going on?" Mrs Shirley said, and she was joined by the oldest lady in the mission, the small and frail-looking Miss Copeland. Miss Copeland was looking from Cordelia to Mrs Clancey with suspicion on her face, and she addressed Cordelia.

"Mrs Entwistle, why were you in this house? Why did you say you were someone else? What have you done to drive this woman here to hurl you onto the street? What, indeed, is your purpose in joining us today? For I do not think you *are* as you seem."

Cordelia did not want to admit that she had lied to the lovely ladies of the mission. That meant she had to say she had lied inside the lodging house. "I think there has been a misunderstanding," she said. "I was looking for a friend of mine, Florence Fry, as I heard she had been cast low and I wished to offer her some assistance if I could. I did not dare to come here alone, so I was able to join the mission, and for that I am grateful. I am deeply sorry I didn't tell you this at the start."

"You said you were some lady thingamabob," Mrs Clancey said. "Hey! Hey!" She began to shout and wave her arms. "Boy, go and fetch that policeman there. Yes, get him over here. Let the law get to the bottom of this, for I cannot be certain that she hasn't stolen anything. Yes. Thief! She must be searched at once, you know. She holds herself most strangely; she must be hiding something on her person."

And that was how Cordelia found herself sitting in a cell of her very own.

CHAPTER NINETEEN

Inspector Hood was clearly loving every minute of it. He had the policeman at the front desk write out a whole list of misdemeanours in a large ledger.

She could console herself, at least, that he did believe she was who she said she was.

He also knew exactly why she had been at the lodging house — "you're trying to play a policeman!" he crowed. "And the landlady thinks you're a thief, to boot."

"You know that I am not."

He grinned widely. "I know nothing of the sort. Why, a woman like you, you might be anything. I must be on my guard. We will have to hold you here while we investigate."

"You should be investigating the murder!"

"We have, and it's done."

"Have you been through that room? Have you examined all areas of it, quite thoroughly?"

"Of course. I assure you, we have taken all the incriminating objects from that place."

"What objects?"

"That is none of your business," he said, shockingly rudely, and had her taken down to a cell.

***

It was unthinkable. She paced around, feeling desperate and furious by equal turns. How had it come to this? And Stanley would still be waiting back at the mission.

She stopped. *Ah, Stanley.* Surely the ladies would tell him what had happened, and he would be able to confirm she was, indeed, Cordelia Cornbrook.

But for the moment, she was trapped, and had to wait.

Well, she thought bitterly, *I am used to this, am I not? Sitting and waiting while other people get on with things in the big wide world.*

Another burst of frustration washed over her, and she went to the bars, and gripped them hard. "Hey! Hey there! I know there is someone out there."

"Yeah, loads of us!" shouted another prisoner, and there was general laughter. A policeman came along to quieten them down, kicking with his boots at the base of the bars.

"You there," she said as the man went past. "I am

Cordelia, Lady Cornbrook."

"I know," he replied. "But law is law, no matter who you are. It is the new way."

"And I agree utterly. But listen, can you get word to a member of my household? They need to know that I am here."

The man paused, and pressed himself up against the cell, sideways, but he remained looking forward. "You really are a lady, are you not?"

"I am. Even Inspector Hood acknowledges that."

"Then it isn't right that you are down here, and you shan't be here long, for I expect he only means to make some sort of example of you, and that's wrong, you know. Who is it that you want to send word to?"

"Anyone, at this address," she said, and told him exactly where she was lodging.

"I shall see to it, my lady, and I am sure they will move you presently."

"Thank you. What is your name?"

"Constable Evans."

And thanks to Constable Evans, a few minutes later she had been released from the cell and allowed to sit in a small, cluttered office, with hazy glass windows that lit out onto a busy corridor.

Inspector Hood opened the door and grinned nastily

at her. "Did you enjoy your little taste of the cells?"

"I did not, but all experience is a learning one, and I thank you for the chance," she said.

"Huh." He slammed the door closed upon her. As soon as he was gone, she jumped up to try the handle but he had locked it.

She didn't sit down again. She paced the small room. It had four cabinets, a bookshelf, a wide desk with many drawers, and two chairs.

She mulled over what she had seen in Mrs Clancey's lodging house. The cupboard's false back was the most obvious thing. She doubted very much that all rooms were so furnished. Did the police know about it?

She wondered if she ought to tell them. But they would ignore her, she was sure of it, and the worse the treatment got that she received from them, the less inclined she was to help them.

No, she resolved. She was on her own, now.

Then she wondered what "objects" had been removed from the room. The wine, obviously; they would have tested it and discovered how it was poisoned. What else?

They wrote everything down, these new police, she remembered. She began to scan the bookshelves and open the cabinet doors.

She had found nothing but lists of names,

incomprehensible figures, and a book on phrenology when the door was flung open again and Inspector Hood yelled out.

"So! You cannot even be trusted in a locked room!"

"There appears to be nothing of interest here, anyway," she said.

"You are correct! There is not! Yet I hoped you might follow common decency as a *lady* by keeping your prying eyes to yourself!" There was spittle at the corner of his mouth, she noticed, and it made her smile as she carefully took her seat once more. She chose the more comfortable chair on the far side of the desk.

"Here. Constable Evans is going to sit here and watch you. And let that be a lesson to you, Evans, about acting without authority."

The young policeman was pushed in and the door locked again behind him. He kept his eyes on the floor as he muttered, "My lady. I have sent word."

"Thank you so much. And I am sorry if it has caused trouble for you."

He shrugged, and took up position by the door, and that was the last of conversation that she was able to draw from him.

She sat and she waited. She imagined overpowering the young constable and kicking her way through the glass out into the corridor. *No,* she thought. *Not with my boots. What else could I use?* She gazed around the room, seeking to make weapons from ordinary objects. *The corner of a heavy-based lamp is a potential cosh,* she thought. *I wonder how I could overpower him? I know that his hat is strengthened against blows, and that his collar is well-starched and upright to guard against the work of the garrotter in the night.*

She was rather enjoying such shameful fantasies when there was a fresh kerfuffle in the corridor. Dark shapes in blue and black moved past the smoked glass.

The office she was being held in was close to the main lobby and there had been many comings and goings, but this was different. It was louder, and she could hear what someone was shouting.

She jumped up and went to the glass. Constable Evans coughed but let her stand there.

She recognised the voice that was making the most noise.

"Hugo Hawke!"

"I shall expose you all in the press!" he was shouting. "You and your colleagues in Holborn. Bow Street is supposed to be better than the rest. I shall expose you. Yes, I shall, you may count on it, sir! Only this morning I was taking breakfast with the editor of a Fleet Street paper."

"All the papers are published in Fleet Street," she heard

Inspector Hood say in a mocking tone. "What are you threatening me with? A paragraph on the back page of 'Pike and Trout Weekly?'"

"Your division's corruption will be the news on every breakfast table in the land!"

She could not help herself. She thought that he must have been nearby when Constable Evans sent to her rented rooms for her staff to be alerted. She began to hammer on the glass. "Mr Hawke! Mr Hawke, I am in here!" She pressed her face against the glass. "It is I, Cordelia! They are keeping me in here!"

There was more shouting and the door was unlocked. Inspector Hood stood there, fury blazing in his eyes. "Madam! If you cannot keep quiet, you shall be returned to the cells."

"But he's here, he's come for me."

"I most certainly have not." Hugo Hawke could not contain his smile as he appeared at Inspector Hood's shoulder. "Well, well. What do you do here?"

"I was waiting for ..."

"Me?"

"Someone."

He began to laugh, and it must have been loud in Inspector Hood's ear, because the policeman shoved Hugo back into the corridor and pulled the door to the office closed again. She started for the door handle but Constable Evans put out his hand to stop her.

"Regretfully, my lady…" he said.

"Of course."

Blast it! She folded her arms and glared at the milky-white glass. She could hear nothing but a low rumble of conversation and passing boots and occasional wordless shouts.

Inspector Hood opened the door again. He was no longer smiling. "Oh, come on then," he said roughly and turned his back on her immediately.

She followed him out into the lobby area where he waved her towards a triumphant-looking Hugo Hawke. He lodged his thumbs in his violently-yellow waistcoat and rocked on his heels. "I was here on another matter entirely," he said. "But it is lucky for you that I was, hey? I have paid the bail for you. Let us go."

"You have…?"

"I have indeed! You may thank me outside."

Some passing policeman made an indelicate remark as to the nature of the thanks that Cordelia might render to Hugo. She hissed at him and stalked out of the police station house. When they got halfway down the stone steps, she grabbed his elbow, and dug her fingernails in sharply.

"You paid my bail?"

"You are being uncommonly slow today, Cordelia. Yes, I have paid for you to be released."

"But look, here is Geoffrey coming for me." The street a few feet below was clogged with traffic. The cab that Geoffrey had commandeered was some way off, and he was half-standing up top next to the driver, waving his arms. As she watched, he leaped down from the cab and began to run, knocking people out of the way.

"He is a little late, your man. And I am disappointed in your ingratitude."

"I never asked you to pay my bail."

"You were hammering on the window and calling for me!"

"Yes, but..."

He grinned widely, with sickly gloating all over his face. "You owe me, Cordelia. You owe me a lot."

CHAPTER TWENTY

Geoffrey was upon them, hurling his bulk along the street, his long black coat flapping behind him. In his right hand was a long whip which he'd clearly stolen from the cab driver.

"Stop!" Cordelia said as Geoffrey drew his hand back. She put out her hands and moved in front of Hugo.

"Saving me from your maniac coachman, that's nice, and I thank you. But it doesn't repay the debt entirely," Hugo said drily.

She ignored him and ran down the remaining three steps to Geoffrey. She almost launched herself into his arms but she stopped short, and instead grabbed hold of the whip, just above his gnarled hand. "Enough!"

"Let me see him off," Geoffrey said.

"All right!" Hugo said. "I am leaving. Good day to you both. And remember, Cordelia … you are in my debt. I shall call." He showed his straight, even teeth, bowed, and lightly ran down the steps at an angle away from them to be swallowed up in the crowd of the streets.

"I am sorry I am so late, my lady," Geoffrey said as he led her back to the cab which had advanced to almost where they stood. "I would have been faster if I had run all the way. We had to stop to pay so many tolls, I suspect the driver to have been going in circles."

"Hoi, sir, you may hand me back my whip this instant!"

"Do it, Geoffrey."

"I had every intention of doing so." Geoffrey sprang up to take his place on the one-person bench next to the driver, though the man was unwilling and nearly pushed him back off again.

"Well, I cannot ride inside with the lady," Geoffrey said, and settled himself over most of the narrow seat. "Back to the Inns, now, if you please."

The journey back was long and bumpy, and Cordelia nestled deep inside the cab, with her eyes half-closed, letting the noise of the wheels and the street beyond lull her into a half-sleep, half-dream.

She played out the room in her head, seeing it from every angle.

Someone broke into the room from the adjoining one, through the cupboard back, she knew. It was too much of a coincidence to ignore it.

Was the back of the cupboard removed that night of the murder?

No, she thought. There was plaster dust on the floor too; between each wardrobe would have been a lath and plaster wall. It would be noisy and have created much more mess than she had seen. So it was pre-meditated.

Had the joiner known?

He had warned her about privacy and security, after all.

Then a new thought struck her. Was, perhaps, Florence — although not guilty of the deed herself — an accomplice? Could she have enticed the man to be there at that time?

Or, more guilty still — did she lay the trap and had she arranged for some other party to come in through the wardrobe and do the deed?

No, she realised. That was nonsense because the manner of killing was poison in the wine. If she was going to poison him, she didn't need anyone to come in from outside.

It meant, even more strongly, that Florence was likely to be innocent of both the crime and the manner of its doing.

Someone must have come in, while they slept, and added the poison to the wine.

And that made Cordelia wonder who the intended victim was. Bonneville, or Florence herself?

Or both?

But Florence did not drink and so she did not die.

Was she still in danger? If so, then the safest place for her to be was probably the police cells, though that was a bit of a stretch, Cordelia had to concur. Surely a small payment in the right hands and anyone could gain access to the cells to end Florence's life.

She remembered Constable Evans. There were still honest men there yet, and too many potential witnesses. No, Florence was as safe there as anywhere.

At least, until they hanged her.

CHAPTER TWENTY-ONE

Cordelia was assailed by the smells of cooking as soon as she entered her sitting room. The door to the kitchen was firmly closed, but it was not enough to prevent the aromas of something sweet wafting through the rest of the rooms. Back at Clarfields, the kitchens were well away from the living areas, down cool corridors and through many doors, to stop the smells contaminating the rest of the house.

But Cordelia quite liked it. She realised that it was mid-afternoon now, and she had not eaten since she had breakfasted on kippers very early in the morning.

There were priorities that came before her stomach, however. "Where is Stanley?" she demanded as she opened the kitchen door.

Mrs Unsworth was by the small range, stirring a copper pot on the top. She simply nodded towards the stable lad who jumped to his feet. He had been sitting at the table, a half-eaten apple in his hands. Judging by the brownness of the apple's flesh, he had been taking his time in eating it.

"My lady!"

"I am glad to see you are back here," she said.

Ruby was also there, and Neville Fry who was polishing the silverware. That was his preferred task when he was distracted and upset. Cordelia wondered if he'd polish the knives right down to mere slivers.

Geoffrey blundered in behind her, and the kitchen was suddenly far too small and far too crowded.

"The ladies of the mission were distressed," Stanley stammered out, bright red, and she felt awful for him.

"I am so, so sorry," she said, wanting to take his hands in hers and reassure him that it didn't matter. But it did matter. "I shouldn't have lied but I didn't think they'd take me seriously if I told them who I really was."

"They can't understand it. They feel betrayed, my lady."

Ruby snorted. But Cordelia put up a warning finger and her maid did not speak.

"I will go to them and make a donation to their works, and try to explain all," she said. "I hope this will not make things awkward for you at your church."

Ruby was unable to stop herself. "They should forgive, though, shouldn't they?"

"They will," Stanley said, but he was miserable. "They

will forgive but they won't forget."

Mrs Unsworth slapped a bowl onto the table and snatched his apple up. "Here, sit, boy. Eat that and stop grizzling." It was as kind as the cook could get, and he sank back to the chair when Cordelia urged him to.

"Now," Cordelia went on. "I have some things to tell you all, especially you, Mr Fry. I think you will be assured that your daughter is, indeed, innocent."

She told them all what she had seen in Mrs Clancey's lodging house. Mrs Unsworth doled out more vermicelli pudding for them all. Geoffrey ate standing up, leaning against a dresser. Ruby and Stanley sat on wooden chairs while a softer one was brought through from the sitting room for Cordelia. She felt deliciously transgressive to be eating with her staff. Neville Fry, of all of them, could not eat in her presence; he simply couldn't unbend enough. Besides, he was hanging on her every word.

She also told them about Hugo Hawke, and how he wanted her help with the police. At that, Geoffrey was immediately suspicious.

"There is a great deal he isn't telling you, my lady."

"I know that, but it intrigues me. He really does seem to need me."

"No. It will be a trick and nothing more. He seeks to bring you down. He'll pretend to be all needful-like, and then at the last minute, he'll sell you out. Avoid him, my lady. Let me go after him, if you like."

"Absolutely not! We've been through this," she said. "You are not to go around hurting people on my behalf. At least, not without my knowledge and permission."

Stanley nodded furiously. She could only see the top of his head and the tips of his ears which were red with anger. *He must be feeling responsible for me being arrested*, she thought, *and therefore responsible for meeting Hugo at the station house.*

But when Stanley spoke, he simply said, "Vengeance is the Lord's." He coughed and dropped his spoon with a clatter, and picked it up with a white-knuckled hand.

Geoffrey said, "Ha! No, it seems to me that vengeance can be the work of man. It saves the Lord some time so He can get on with other stuff. Like, oh, inventing giraffes and all that. Singing on clouds."

"That's angels," Ruby said, but she was laughing.

Even Mrs Unsworth seemed to stir the pot with a slightly lighter hand and Cordelia herself smiled.

They all froze when they heard a knock on the outer door. It persisted and grew louder.

Neville Fry suddenly roused himself and patted at his trousers and jacket and tried to smooth his hair down, all at the same time. "The door!" he said, as if no one had realised.

"Go to it, please."

He disappeared, through the sitting room and into the antechamber that lay between the main rooms and the corridor. She heard a familiar voice.

"It's Septimus," she said. "I'll meet him in the sitting room. Thank you for the pudding, Mrs Unsworth."

The cook grunted.

Cordelia walked into the sitting room still carrying a little mirth in her heart, which curled up and died as soon as she saw Septimus's long face. He folded his arms and she knew that gesture from her girlhood. He'd always seemed old, to her, and now she felt like a little girl again, caught running through the flowerbeds or teaching the dog to roll over and play dead when someone sneezed.

"I have heard of your latest exploits," he said.

"Ahh. Um, do have a seat, dear Septimus."

He hesitated long enough to make her feel awkward, and then flung himself into a wing-backed chair. He stretched out his long legs and crossed them at the ankles. "Cordelia. Explain."

"What exactly have you heard?" she countered.

"Why, does that make a difference to what you are about to explain? Is your version of the truth dependent on what I want or need to hear? Are you going to lie to me like you have done to the good and honest ladies of East Street Mission?"

Cordelia folded herself into a chair opposite him. "I did not mean to take advantage of their good natures..."

"But you did. So, explain, if you will, for you are here trading on *my* good name and *my* good nature and if you have used me in this manner also..."

"No! Not at all! Listen..."

She told Septimus everything she had previously told her staff. He listened, and he softened as he did so. She was glad to see it. She could not bear the thought of having her old friend disappointed in her.

"I can understand your actions," he said at last. "I don't agree with them, not one bit, but I know you, and I can see how you ended up acting so ... impulsively."

"That is a kind way of saying I am a foolish woman."

He raised an eyebrow, and allowed her a brief smile. But he soon returned to a more serious tone. "Unfortunately, Cordelia, there are wider ramifications of your actions. I am not here to be kind. Have you not yet wondered how I came to hear of these misadventures?"

"I have ... and I assume that the streets of London are already paved with gossip rather than gold."

"Indeed they are. The police sell their stories to the newspapers, obviously, and I work in the world of publishing. And nothing travels faster than news. A meeting here, a word there, a mention over a drink … I suspect I know more about the situation than you do."

"How so?"

"I know, for example, that you are not to be charged with anything. The police have had their sport, and now it is over."

She felt relief wash over her, sweat prickling all along her spine. "Oh! Thank goodness."

"Alas, that is not quite the end of it for you. Or, in another sense, it is very much an ending…"

"Septimus, enough with the riddles, please!"

"I hesitate to tell you this." He sighed. "I am sorry. I cannot put it off. Cordelia, the magazine has cancelled your column."

"What?"

"No more weekly articles on cookery or anything. I am sorry. You were already on thin ice because you were not writing exactly the sort of thing that the readers wanted. Then you missed a deadline. And now this scandal — they simply can't keep you on."

"But…" She subsided into a gloomy silence. There was no point in arguing. She knew why the magazine could not continue to publish her. It would be death to their sales.

Septimus got to his feet and extended his hands. She

rose, dutifully, and he enfolded in a sudden, surprising, deeply improper hug. She hadn't been held in so long — so many years — that the shock of the contact with another human body nearly broke her. She swallowed painfully and blinked until her eyes were clear again. He squeezed, and then released her.

"I take the liberty as I once saw you quite naked," he said, daringly. "Admittedly, you were three years old at the time."

"Septimus, thank you."

"Please, Cordelia, have a think about what your aims are to be, now. I honestly counsel you to give up the writing."

"My aim is to solve this murder."

She waited for him to try and dissuade her.

He did not.

"Then I wish you all the luck in the world, and you know where I am if you need to call on me and my resources at any time."

He left, and Cordelia sank back into the chair. She closed her eyes for a brief moment. When the door from the kitchen opened slightly, she barked at whoever it was to leave her alone; she didn't open her eyes but she heard the door close again.

She was morose about the column.

But she had an aim, and she had support, and those

things were beyond value. How many other widows in her position had such motivation in their lives, save for the endless quest to find ones' self a new husband?

Refocus, refocus, she told herself. *I must look again at that lodging house with the false wardrobe. Someone has done that; someone will know. Did that joiner know anything of it? If he did, then he was foolish to let me into that room. At any rate, I must return there, somehow.*

And Socks. They say that he was an enemy of Bonneville yet there was a connection there. The connection is Florence Fry. She groaned in frustration. How could she get to see Albert Socks? He haunted clubs and dining rooms; places she could not go.

He was single, as far as she could tell. No one spoke of a wife or a family. Ruby had confirmed it from her dealings at the house, speaking to the staff there.

She was startled once more by a knocking at the outer door. She thought it would be Septimus, returned to tell her some new thing or to collect something he might have left behind, so she sprang to the antechamber and answered the door herself.

It was not Septimus Gibbs.

The smug, slappable face of Hugo Hawke leered at her. He leaned his weight on one leg, posing and louche, and said, "Hello again, dear Cordelia. This is merely a courtesy call to see if you are quite recovered after your earlier ordeal."

"I should slam this door in your face."

He shoved out a booted foot against the door. "You should let me in. Do not forget, *dear* one. You owe me."

CHAPTER TWENTY-TWO

She backed into the sitting room. "All my staff are here, including Geoffrey." She nodded towards the kitchen door. She didn't think he would try anything, but she was taking no risks.

"Jolly good." Hugo ignored her veiled threat, and instead wandered around the room, staring idly at the pictures on the walls.

"Oh, sit down. If you are trying to unsettle me, it's not working. You're just annoying," she snapped.

"Ooh, but you sound unsettled." Nevertheless, he took the winged armchair that Septimus had just vacated. She hoped, viciously, that it was still unpleasantly warm.

She remained standing, and placed herself close to the door to the kitchen. With her arms folded, she said, "I am fine. Thank you for coming. Thank you for paying my bail. How much was it? I shall settle up with you immediately."

He waved at her dismissively. "No need, no need. You can pay me in other ways."

"Geoffr—"

"No, no, no, foolish woman. You do think very lowly of me, don't you? I can admit I am a cad, but I am not that beastly. No, I want information. What have you found out about the police?"

"I don't really understand what you want."

"Evidence, hard evidence, that they are corrupt and ignoble curs so that I might have them all dismissed and … and *honest* men put in their place."

"I cannot think of a single bit of hard evidence that would suit your purpose. What do you want? A signed confession? There is much that you are not telling me." She wanted to stamp her feet in frustration. "You ask the impossible of me!"

"Listen, while you were in the station house, did any of the policemen there seem likely to be honest? Were there any who might speak privately to you? Anybody upon whom you might use your womanly charms? Anyone who might turn evidence against the malpractice in that division, or others? Bow Street is important. I think that might be my way in to expose Holborn."

She thought immediately of Constable Evans. She said, "No. No one would speak to me."

He sighed. "I should have left you there. I wonder if I can get you re-arrested…"

"Absolutely not!"

He smoothed down his whiskers and sighed again. If he did it a third time, she resolved to throw something at his head. He said, "Perhaps we need to make allies in other areas. I must have my way into this pit of snakes. I must stop them!"

"And this is all to do with your public house, is it?"

"You don't believe me?"

"No, I shall be frank with you: I do not!"

"The police are stopping my boxing matches unless I pay them vast bribes. This is blackmail, plain and simple. I told you this."

"These boxing matches of yours, Hugo. Are they fixed? Are they legal?"

"Of course they are not fixed. They're a vital source of revenue, it is true. But all manner of men attend them, even fine gentlemen. It's not just a sport for the lower orders, though there is a certain element of 'roughing it' that appeals to gentlemen and the like."

She noted that he had not answered her query as to the legality of the matches. She filed that away.

"Tell me this," she said. "Have you heard of one Lord Brookfield? Does he attend them?"

"I have heard of the man, of course, but no, I am unaware of him attending the matches. My publican would have told me, I am sure of it. He keeps me appraised of the more interesting spectators."

"What about the man who is dead, Bonneville?"

"Again, I know him by reputation only."

"Well, then. And what of one Albert Socks?"

"Oh, that reprobate?" He laughed. "What do you want with him? I meet him at card games around the city from time to time. Is he a suspect in your little endeavour?"

"He is certainly of interest to my enquiries," she said.

"Aha! And you want an introduction to him, I suppose? Another favour from me, eh? They are quite stacking up."

She narrowed her eyes at him. "It could be for your benefit too."

"How?"

"There was one constable at the station house who might look favourably on me."

"You said there was not!"

"I am not certain. I didn't want to get your hopes up."

"You were playing with me. You must trust me, Cordelia."

"As you trust me?"

They paused for a moment in a mutual appreciation

of the impasse. Then Hugo said, "Right. Well, you are something of a card shark yourself, I remember. Devilishly good at holding and hiding a hand. So, if you want to meet this man, why not challenge him to a game?"

"It could work, if you could effect an introduction."

"And then," Hugo went on, mocking her now. "I am sure that you will win, and your cunning skills will so unnerve him that he will confess all, and you will have your murderer, and that will prove the police have the wrong culprit, and that will help me to expose them. Is that how you think this will work?"

"Not entirely."

Hugo sprang to his feet. "No, wait, I have it. I will be hiding in a secret place during the card game. You will beat him, and he will be a broken, shamed man. He will confess, and I will spring from the hiding place and take him to the police who will have to confess that you are right and they are wrong, and so their superintendent and all his cronies will have to resign, and then I can install my own man, and— what?"

Cordelia glared at him. "Your own man?"

He blustered and he huffed but now she was sure this was about more than the blackmail and bribery of the police. He wanted more than just the go-ahead for his own boxing matches. He was corrupt, and she had always really known it.

Before she could challenge him, he spun around on his heel and strode up to her, closer than she was comfortable with. "Right," he said. "I will get you close to Socks. I will arrange a meeting. No, not a card game. And I will do it discreetly. I assume that you do not want me to expose your interest in this man?"

"No, I do not."

"Well, then. I will do this for you, and you will make contact again with your friendly policeman, and you will help me to bring them all down. Is it a deal?"

She did not want to agree. But this was her only chance. She opened her mouth to ask if he knew of any connections with Mrs Clancey's lodging house — was it a common place for politicians to meet their mistresses, that sort of thing — but she swallowed her questions. She did not want Hugo to know too much about her investigation. He already knew more than he needed to.

"It is a deal," she said through gritted teeth. "Now, go."

He left, and she stamped through into the kitchen, nearly knocking over her staff like a heap of skittles.

"You are not even pretending that you weren't listening at the door!" she said angrily.

Only Stanley had the decency to look contrite.

194

CHAPTER TWENTY-THREE

In the far corner of the dining room, a woman was singing a plaintive tune. In all other respects, the eating house superficially was a decent one, but the singer made it have something of a saloon bar feel, or like a low-brow musical theatre. *Such things might be fashionable in Paris,* Cordelia thought, *but had they really become so current here in London?*

Certainly, as she looked around, there was a good mix of well-bred folks. But there were hints at less savoury characters, too. There was a woman who was a good deal older than the man she was with. There was another man, a finely dressed gentleman, with two identical young women to either side of him. His manner of interacting with them suggested — or one hoped — that they were not his daughters.

And here she was, dining out, almost in public, with

the minor politician, Albert Socks.

Scandal would surely follow.

She stole another glance at him and cringed inside. *How on earth did Florence bear it?* She could not spend much longer in his company, even if her life depended on it.

The food was excellent, and worthy of any classier dining room or private club. The wine, likewise, was of the very best quality. The staff were dignified and unobtrusive, and the furnishings were light and glittery, sparkling as they reflected the lights and lamps of the high-ceilinged room.

They were tucked away on a small, round table. All of the areas were discreet and half-hidden, and Cordelia was grateful. This had been Hugo's choice of meeting area, and he assured her that she would be quite safe. She had expected him to arrange a private room in an inn, perhaps. Not this edge-of-society place. When he had told her she would be safe, she had imagined he meant safe from gossip and prying eyes.

But the understated attentiveness of the waiters hovering around were the real key to her security, and Hugo must have known that. In a private room, she would have been at this man's mercy completely. She had everything to fear from the man she was with.

"How is your pigeon, dear? Mine seems a little overdone."

"In truth, it is perfect," she said, though she wished she hadn't had as much soup in the preceding course. There was quite a lot of food still to get through.

Albert Socks' lower lip was red and pendulous and it shone with the continual flicking of his tongue as he wetted it. His eyes were bright blue rimmed by pink, with pale eyelashes and a limp brown-blond hair that was neither light nor dark nor mid-toned. The best thing one could say of his hair was that it was plentiful.

As unprepossessing as his visage was, his manner was worse, at least to Cordelia's mind. She wondered if she was judging him unfairly, based on her preconceived assumptions as to his possible guilt in the murder.

Then she felt something press against her ankle under the table, and she withdrew her legs sharply. How he had managed to snake his own foot past her petticoats was a feat in itself; he must be practised at it.

She reminded herself of her purpose. She needed to unpick his relationship with Florence, the Lord Brookfield and, indeed, the dead Louis Bonneville.

"I am so grateful to you for bringing me here," she said. She dredged up all she had ever learned of acting the coquette and making light, idle conversation. "Since I arrived here in London, why, I have not stopped! I have been here, there and everywhere. This ball, that soiree, the other gathering … it is so delicious to be able to simply sit and converse with someone."

He smiled and met her eyes, holding her gaze. She let him stare, though she soon felt uncomfortable. "My dear, the pleasure is all mine. But do you really tire of gaiety and life?"

"Well, I find I need to withdraw and rest from time to time. But no, I shall never tire of dancing!" She laughed and hoped she didn't sound like a braying donkey with its tail trapped in a gate.

"I should love to see you dance," he murmured. "I imagine you are like a fine thoroughbred."

In that I could kick you in the head and run off very quickly, she thought. *Yes, that fits.* She smiled and looked down as if she were flattered. "Do you know," she said, "I think we have a connection in common."

"We are bound to have!" he said. "You are a titled lady, and I am a man of some repute."

She was not titled, and carried the "lady" as a relic of her dead husband's status only, but she did not correct him. She said, "My butler's daughter, Florence Fry, she was an employee of yours, was she not?"

Socks was good at hiding his feelings, except that his tongue ran over his lip a little more frantically. Other than that, his face was impassive. "Oh, yes, I had a maid of that name. They come and they go. Indeed, I regret to say that she was not all she seems … you know, I suppose, of her unfortunate fate? I hope your butler is not of the same ilk. Watch him. It is usually in the blood, you know."

"She was not always so," Cordelia said. "I feel for her. We women are not born bad, I promise you!"

"Yet Eve…"

"Oh, hush." She lightly tapped the back of his hand, and he looked at her with a seductive cast to his eyes. "No, I cannot countenance that. It is my understanding that poor Florence was quite the innocent, once. I wonder. Before she came to you, she was in the service of another — a Lord Brookfield. And you know of him, I think?"

"Oh, um, old Brookfield, yes, our paths do cross from time to time."

"Perhaps it was he who … oh, I am sorry." She clapped her hand over her mouth as if she had said too much. Then she thought she might be over-egging the drama somewhat, and let her hand fall. "Forgive me. Are you two friends with one another, perhaps?"

She watched him intently. He blustered and then gave a hearty laugh but when he spoke, his voice had an edge of uncertainty. "Well, no, I would not say that, no. We share common goals within the party, I think you might say. Oh, that's politics, of no interest to a lady such as yourself, of course."

No, she thought, *I am only interested in needlework and giggling.* "And are you an ambitious man?"

"Of course! Any real man wishes to rise to the very peak of his profession, does he not? Ah, you ladies have it most easy in life. You are not sent out into the dirty world to claw one's way to the top."

She smiled thinly but it wasn't as if he was saying anything she had not heard before. "More wine?" she suggested.

And so it went. He drank heavily and his foot probed beneath the table, and her skirts, with clumsy abandon. She took to kicking him quite sharply and he seemed to count such violence as mere flirting.

They ploughed their way through more courses, and she let him rabbit on about his ambitions. She tried to steer him to talk about relationships: "And surely you need a wife? You cannot work hard all day and come home to an empty house..."

"Oh, I live quite the social whirl," he said. "Of course in good time I shall choose a wife but there is no hurry."

Cordelia begged to differ, but she kept her uncharitable thought to herself. He wasn't a looker even now, and time was not going to be kind to him. Obviously, he thought that money and power would be enough to net him a pretty woman.

She had to concede that he might be right about that.

She tried to steer the conversation to his relationship with Lord Brookfield, but he was not to be led. She didn't think that he was artfully evading her any longer; he simply couldn't hold a meaningful conversation. She probed him about Bonneville, trying to sound as if she were a mere gossip, but he reacted dramatically.

"Oh, no, dear lady, not again; I cannot bear it!" He pushed his half-eaten pudding to one side. It was an impressive display of red and yellow custards in layers, with jelly and thin slices of gold leaf and almonds set into it. She resisted the urge to snatch it from him; she'd politely opted for a stewed pear and was regretting her dietary restraint.

"But this murder is the most exciting thing to have happened!" she said, wincing as she heard her own words.

"It is all *too* troubling and *too* close to home," he said. "I mean with that girl being the murderer. Honestly! I can barely keep my staff from one month to the next, and when I do, they turn out to be murderers. I really am the unluckiest man when it comes to finding decent domestics."

"But what if Florence is innocent?" she said.

"Inconceivable," he said flatly. "She was there. And she should not have been there. She was in my service."

"It was in a lodging house, in a rented room, was it

not? I believe it read it," she said, carefully. She didn't want him to know that she already knew some facts. If, indeed, Florence had been telling the truth about the room.

"So I believe," Socks said, as if he didn't really know. "Some terrible cheap place somewhere." He affected a shudder. "No, I shall not think of her nor speak of her again."

His face was red now, and his eyes were growing smaller. She did not want to push him into anger. She encouraged him to finish his glass and order another.

Her aim now was to get him drunk enough that he fell asleep, so that she could ask the maître d' to call her a cab.

And the sooner the better.

CHAPTER TWENTY-FOUR

Cordelia woke early the next morning. The day was not full of the spring-like promise that she had hoped for. It was grey and dank, with a light drizzle which made the sitting room gloomy. She sank into her armchair, wrapped in a housecoat, and asked Ruby to make up a small fire. The maid clicked her tongue at the extravagance.

"I need something to look at while I order my thoughts," Cordelia explained. "There is too much whizzing around in my head. I need to make sense of my meal last night with Albert Socks. He was an odious man, you know."

"So I understand. His staff have no love for him," Ruby said as she bustled around. She brought in some thin sticks from the kitchen and began to lay them out in the grate.

Cordelia didn't reply. Her head was somewhat thick and fuzzy from the overindulgence of the previous evening, and she had only risen from bed because she was thirsty. Once up, she decided she would stay up.

Three hours later, and she was finally dressed and had breakfasted though it had technically been lunch, and had resumed her place in the chair by the fire, when Ivy Delaney arrived on a morning call. She was early as it had only just gone midday. Neville Fry leaped at the chance to do something and answered the door. Cordelia heard the now-familiar voice of the magistrate's wife enquiring if Cordelia was "at home" and she jumped to her feet. She hadn't given Neville any orders so she was afraid he would turn Ivy away. She popped her head into the lobby.

"Dear Ivy! Please, come in. A tea-tray if you will, please, Mr Fry. Perhaps some light snacks."

"At once, my lady."

They got themselves settled quickly. Neville efficiently set up a small table in between two comfortable chairs at the fire, and Ivy perched on hers, hampered slightly by her very fashionable skirts. Cordelia had decided to cling to the older styles and blame it on her widowhood. She sat back, teacup in hand. They exchanged a few pleasantries, and discussed the weather for the minimum acceptable amount of time.

"I am glad you have a fire lit," Ivy said. "My Anthony would not countenance it between the months of March and October."

"I am grateful to be the mistress of my own house. Oh, if you are hot, please ignore formality and remove your gloves if you wish. I shall tell no one."

"Are you not lonely?"

Cordelia forgave Ivy's impulsiveness. "Not yet, as I have not had the time."

Ivy smiled. "Now, listen, my dear, for I am here on an important matter. At least, I think it is important. It is certainly odd. Not all odd things are important, of course, but..."

Cordelia sipped at her tea.

"I am sorry! I do run on so. You must tell me to stop and gather my thoughts. My old governess would slap a cane across the back of my hands. That usually worked."

"Have you brought a cane?"

"Well, no, I rather feel I have grown beyond quite such ... oh, you jest." But Ivy took the teasing in good stead. "Where was I? Ah! The visitor."

"Which visitor?"

"A man came to see my Anthony this morning, rather early. Too early, if you ask me, so of course Anthony received him, for if someone feels compelled to call at such an hour, then there must be something very important about the call, don't you think?"

"Indeed," said Cordelia.

"Now ordinarily I would not be party to these things but as soon as the man had left, Anthony called me in, because he knows that I have visited you."

"Mm-hm?"

"My dear, I fully support your investigation, for it is both exciting and morally correct. But, and I hate to try to advise you, but you are an innocent here, so I feel that I must, but — do be careful not to go out and ask questions directly of people."

"I have totally lost the thread of this conversation," Cordelia said. "Is that what the visitor said? Who was this visitor?"

"Oh! Of course. This man who came, he was asking questions about you, you see."

"Me?"

"Indeed, he mentioned you by name, and asked what connection you had to the case, and what capacity you were acting in. We were both most concerned! And so you see, you ought to be a little careful about how you go about this. You can most effectively use your mind from a distance, and consider the facts in cold objectivity. There is no need for you to chase about in the world, like a common detective."

"I need to seek out the facts first before I can consider

them," Cordelia said.

"Discreetly, dear, discreetly. Oh, and this man, he had the most curious name. Socks! What do you make of that? I am fascinated by the history of one's surname; Cornbrook is easy, of course, and did you know that Delaney is Irish and originates from something rather unpronounceable?"

"Albert Socks!" Cordelia said, refusing to be distracted by Ivy's conversational detours.

"Yes, and what is more, he was trying to put pressure on my Anthony to bring the trial of that poor girl forwards!"

"Is that so?"

"I know! I can barely believe it myself. Of course, my Anthony is approached by all manner of people all the time, with this demand and that demand. He is used to it. He told this fellow, quite firmly, that it must go to the monthly court at the Old Bailey. The man even insinuated that he could give my Anthony money for the trial to happen this week instead of next month! But my Anthony isn't even connected with this case."

"You are a good woman and you are married to a very good man," Cordelia said. "Thank you so much for coming to me with this information. For, you know, it does help to stack the case up against this Albert Socks."

"Do you know the man?"

"Indeed I do. I was dining with him last night."

Shock and horror crept over Ivy's face. "And yet he came to our house this morning ... oh, goodness, is he a suspect?"

"He is my primary suspect at the moment," Cordelia said.

Ivy's eyes were round and full of life. "How terribly exciting!" she said.

"More cake?"

* * *

After Ivy had left, brimming with excitement and sweet pastries, Cordelia went to the kitchens. Her servants had adopted the room as their day room, although Mrs Unsworth was not delighted about the fact. She had absented herself again, and no one knew where she was. Cordelia gave leave for Stanley to go out, and Geoffrey was already established in a local alehouse.

Neville Fry dashed into the sitting room to find things to polish, which left Cordelia alone in the kitchen with Ruby. She was sitting on the long wooden bench at the table, paring apples and putting them in a wide beige bowl.

Cordelia prowled around the kitchen, examining cupboards and opening packets. As she meandered, she filled Ruby in with the latest developments. In truth, she was talking as much to herself as to the maid. It helped to organise her thoughts.

"This Albert Socks, he's full of ambition. And guilt! I can see it but I cannot yet prove it. I must find out where he was on the night of the murder. Did he rent the room next to the room that Bonneville died in? That would fit! Yes, if he had rented two rooms there, not just one..."

Ruby concentrated on peeling each apple in one long, unbroken curl.

"He had lost his woman to Bonneville. I wonder if he knew about that? If he had found out, well, there's a motive. And for Florence to use that very room that Socks had given her! And did you not say that Socks and Bonneville hated one another? Oh, for him to lose his woman to a man he despised ... the motives just stack up and up!"

"And the manner of killing?" Ruby said at last. "Poisoning is a woman's crime. Wouldn't he rather had called Bonneville out?"

"The man is too flabby to fight anyone," Cordelia said. "And anyway, Socks would have known that Florence could not drink. So by poisoning the wine, not only did he ensure only Bonneville died, but it gave him a scapegoat too! By having the blame land so squarely on Florence, no one would think to look any further. And so it has been proved!"

"Then he must have found out about Florence and Bonneville," Ruby said.

"Yes. I wonder how he knew when and where they

would be meeting? For the manner of killing was planned in advance," Cordelia said. She peeked in chest that was on the floor by the range. "Flour?"

"I believe so, to keep dry."

"Hmm." She ran her fingers through the light powder. "Ruby, I need evidence. I must act. Ivy means well, by saying I should keep myself closeted up and simply *think* about things. But I cannot. I know I have got myself into some scrapes, but I will be more careful."

Ruby put her knife down and looked up, an expression of resignation on her face. "Really? I do not want to pick up the papers to find some wonderful story about your kidnapping, or worse."

"Of course you don't. You'd hate to have to go to the effort of finding a new situation."

Ruby sighed and picked up another apple to peel. "If I throw this over my shoulder, it should make the shape of the initial letter of the man I am destined to marry," she said.

"As long as he is called Stephen, Seth or Stuart, I suppose."

"Indeed. My lady, you ought to be careful, it is true. But above that, you ought to be *clever*."

"You are quite right, Ruby. Quite right."

Cordelia continued her exploration of the kitchen.

From time to time, she took a small item from a shelf or a cupboard, and stowed it carefully away in her large bag.

CHAPTER TWENTY-FIVE

This soiree was darker. The laughter was louder and the music seemed discordant as one moved from room to room. The rousing, bouncing arpeggios of the strings were distorted by the pillars and doors and walls and ceilings, echoing off the wood panelling and being absorbed by the thick velvet curtains.

"They could stand to light more lamps in here," Cordelia hissed to Septimus Gibbs. They had danced, though she had found her feet to be sluggish and unwilling. Now they were lingering in a smaller side room, one of the many that opened out along the long side of a great hall. The hall itself was given over to dancing. She watched the twirling satins and silks flash by, set out like jewels against the black and white of the men's formal suits.

"I rather suspect that the Duke is less wealthy than he'd like to appear," Septimus murmured back, after a quick glance around to check that they were not overheard bad-mouthing their host.

"Still," she said, "I do thank you for obtaining this invitation at such short notice."

"My dear, whenever I receive a note from you, I simply spring into action."

"Hmm." The double doors were pressed back and she went to the open doorway to scan the dancing crowd again. "There is no sign of him, Septimus!"

He came to her side. "I am sorry. I had heard strong rumour that the Lord Brookfield would be here, but there was never any certainty. Strong rumour is yet just rumour."

"I must speak with him again! I must befriend him."

"Is he quite central to your enquiry?"

"I wish to dig deeper into his relationship with Albert Socks. Socks is my primary suspect, however."

"As far as I know, from what you have said, there is no relationship," he reminded her.

"One, or both of them, is lying. I can feel it! I would like to say that it is down to my womanly intuition, but it is more than that. Their words do not add up. He has a secret. He knows Socks well enough to have passed Florence on to him. Oh, Septimus. I need more champagne."

"I would suggest, my dearest Cordelia, that you do not."

She drew herself up to her full height, and looked him in the eyes. "If the Lord Brookfield does not turn up, I may as well get roaring drunk and go home and sleep it all off," she said.

"I would advise you to stay relatively sober."

She glared.

He merely looked at her mildly, with a paternalistic air.

"Please," she pleaded. "I shall not embarrass you. We all have a weakness and anyway, why should I not relax a little?"

He pressed his lips together but he acquiesced in the end. He went to find a nearby waiter and obtain another glass for her.

***

Lord Brookfield appeared when Cordelia least expected it. She had talked with a few other people. There was a woman from her own finishing school who had been married for nearly fifteen years now, and the knowledge made Cordelia feel old and rather tired. She drank another glass to perk herself up. Then there was a missionary, lately returned from thrilling adventures in the colonies. She had gone out there with her husband, and come back a widow and with a shaking sickness that came in waves, rendering her helpless for days, but the attacks were predictable and so she planned her social calendar around them. She also spoke with a few dashing young cavalry officers who were full of life and plans and who had never waved a sword anywhere but the training grounds of their regiment. She drank to their health and hoped they lived long enough to look back on their boastful words with regret.

So when the tall, distinguished figure of Lord Brookfield finally entered the room, at a very late hour, she was feeling hot and droopy and loud and sad, all at the same time. She knew she had taken too much alcohol, and it had split her good sense off from the rest of her personality. Her common sense was now in a glass cage, watching with horror as the drunk, uninhibited Cordelia walked unsteadily up to Lord Brookfield and tapped his arm like a coquette.

"Sir! At last! I have been waiting for you!"

He gazed down at her with dark eyes. "Indeed? I do apologise, then, for my tardiness. I had three other engagements this evening. I feel spread rather thin, I am afraid."

"Let us hope they have not taken the best of you!" she said. *Goodness,* she thought, *it almost sounds as if I am flirting.*

"There is very little of me that could be called the best anyway," he said. He smiled and she hoped it was not because he was simply humouring her. "I am old, and my best was long ago."

She stopped herself. She was about to say "I am sure

there is life in the old dog yet" and not only was that a cliché, it was most *definitely* flirting. She worked hard to get a grip on her tongue, and to remember her task. She was to befriend him, and work out his secret; not to present herself as a jade and earn his scorn.

"And yet what of the future?" she said at last. "For you are a political man, and you work for the good of the nation. How very hard it is, and how very magnanimous you must be, that you work for a future that — forgive me — is far ahead."

"A future that I may never see?" he said, amused.

"Well, I do not quite mean to say it like that," she said, stumbling. She never did have the easy way with words that other women seemed to have. The to-and-fro of frothy light conversation had ever eluded her, and with the influence of alcohol in her blood, she was finding it doubly difficult. "Still, it's rather like planting trees, I would imagine."

He looked surprised and thought about that for a moment before he smiled. "Indeed, I suppose it is. Yes, do they not say that anyone who plants a tree is blessed? For only his great-great-grandchildren will enjoy the shade."

"How lovely and how poignant," she said.

"But, enough of this. The last time that we met, my dear lady, we spoke then of politics too. My work is tedious work. But what of yourself?" His eyes seemed to twinkle and she had a horrible feeling that she knew what he was about to say next.

And he said it. "What of yourself? As a widow, I understand that you are submerging yourself in most estimable charitable endeavours. Which is only to be praised, of course."

He was referring, in a most roundabout fashion, to the escapade at Mrs Clancey's lodging house.

She said, "I am, alas, flawed in too many ways and perhaps I ought to offer myself up as a recipient of the East Street Ladies' Mission, rather than as a do-gooder myself."

He sipped at his glass. She matched him, out of politeness. The desire to drink was leaving her but there was nothing else to do with her hands.

"I thought you were here in London to soak up the culture?" he said.

"I was, I mean, I am. Do you attend concerts?"

"Rarely."

"Or the opera? Or galleries? Can you recommend any exhibitions that are showing that I might find improving?"

"Sadly, no. I do keep myself to myself, for the most part. I am sure you think me awfully dull."

"And yet this is your third, no, fourth engagement of the evening!"

"Duty, alas, not pleasure. It is my duty to be seen."

Much like Gibbs, then, she thought. *Huh, I thought it was only us women who had a duty to be looked at and admired.*

But this was still getting her nowhere. She drained her glass as frustration made her ache. The last time she had spoken with him, she had mentioned Albert Socks and he had given her the impression — truthfully or artfully — that he was not close to the man.

She had not, however, mentioned Florence Fry that time.

She hadn't intended to bring the young woman into the conversation overtly but she could not see how to be subtle in her probing. Perhaps it was best to simply come straight out with it. She noticed that he was looking around, as if growing bored of her company. Already the party was dwindling as people went home, or on to other places.

"And what is your opinion, as a learned man, on the strange business of the awful murder of your fellow politician?" she blurted out.

He tipped his head back and stared down his aquiline nose at her. "Strange business? I do not see it was so strange. That girl was there in the room, and so was he. Dead, alas."

"If she had done it, she would have run away," Cordelia pointed out, feeling a spark of triumph. She decided that she sounded quite natural in her conversation. *He won't suspect a thing.*

"And what do you know of it, beyond the newspapers?"

"Well, it is quite the topic of conversation, is it not? And everyone knows she was found in the room, and that is most suspicious, to my mind, for any murderer with half an ounce of sense would have made themselves scarce."

"But there is the rub. Murderers are not known for their sense, or they would not be murdering, would they? She was quite insensible when they found her."

"Drunk?"

"I believe not, but she was asleep or generally incapable."

Cordelia chewed on her lip. *So he knew she did not drink, then,* she thought. *Incapable? I need to know more.* "The girl was in the employ, if we can call it that, of one of your contemporaries, Albert Socks."

He spun his now-empty glass between his long fingers. She watched it obsessively, expecting him to lose his grip and drop it at any moment. "You mentioned that man once before to me. I have an exceedingly good memory, you know. It is essential in my line of work."

"Did I?" She tried to giggle innocently. Her mouth was dry and she ended up coughing.

"You did. And you never did explain why you had an

interest in him."

"Oh, I am interested in all manner of people. Like Florence, for instance..."

"Florence?"

Cordelia bit on her tongue. She had used the name with too familiar a tone, and he had picked up on it instantly. "That is the girl who they have accused, is it not? Florence Fry."

"Indeed it is. Miss Fry seems a sad sort of fallen woman. I am sure, with your charitable works, you would agree with me that such people need our help and sympathy. Though in this case, she is beyond any earthly redemption."

"But why did she not run away after the act? And why would she kill the man, anyway?" Cordelia said, almost petulantly. She knew she was on dangerous ground. She wanted to stamp her feet. She felt as if there was something very obvious that she was missing, and she was beginning to feel desperate. She was drunk, and tired, and fed up, and events were going to overwhelm her unless she got a grip.

She would *not* have hysterics. Not here in public, not in private, not ever.

But sometimes, the idea of having a screaming, weeping meltdown was so very tempting.

"My good lady..." he said, and his tone was gentle. "You seem vexed. Do not take it to heart."

"But I fear there has been a mistake!" she burst out.

He was, in truth, a complete gentleman, and he did his best to follow the rules of polite conversation. It was she who was causing the problems. "Forgive me," she said, feeling more and more fuzzy-headed. "It is very late."

"It is. Are you quite well? Might I call for some water? Here, let me lead you to a chair…"

She could not argue back. She accepted his arm and he steered her to a peaceful corner. "I will be back directly," he said.

She nodded gratefully. He slipped away and she admired his upright back as he disappeared from view.

She knew that she should leave the party. The rooms were almost empty now. She leaned to one side, supported by her corset, and let her head rest against the wall. It was cool to her skin and she realised how hot and flustered she was.

When Lord Brookfield returned, he was accompanied by Septimus. Her old friend had a worried frown. "Cordelia! I have been looking out for your boy who is to collect you but there is no sign of him. Was he not to wait here with the hired carriage?"

"He was. He should be about, and the carriage at the back."

"I have checked the servants' hall, and the courtyard,

and the stables," Gibbs said.

"He will be back soon. It is only a little fly that he is in, with a chestnut mare. Perhaps he is on a little tour of the streets. Who knows what is in the boy's head. We arranged that he would meet me at the front around midnight."

She took the glass of water from Lord Brookfield and thanked him. He nodded and peeled away. She knew that he would want to distance himself from her and her apparent instability. She did not notice where he went; instead she blinked blearily at Septimus.

"Do not worry, Septimus."

"But I must worry," he said. "I have to leave now; I have a game to attend to, and I promised I should be there."

"So late?"

"Indeed. My friend Alfred is a poet, and something of a night owl, and his poker games are legendary. I must not delay. But I cannot leave you here like this."

"Of course you can! Go, go. I am in the Duke's house, and quite safe. As soon as Stanley arrives, I will be informed of it, and I will go home."

Septimus dithered, but eventually he was persuaded to leave.

Cordelia drank the water, and watched the house gradually empty. She rested for nearly half an hour. That was plenty of time for Stanley to return.

Her mind, too, began to clear from the effects of alcohol, though her head seemed to be spinning just a little too much for comfort. Finally she sought out the Duke, complimented him on his gathering, took her leave and went to await Stanley in the cool night air outside. There was a short driveway and a high wall that screened the house from the quiet London road beyond; they were in an exclusive area, here, and all was peaceful.

There was still no sign of Stanley.

CHAPTER TWENTY-SIX

The moon was a sliver high in the sky, glowing very faintly behind scudding grey clouds. The air seemed thick. In winter, it was worse; then, great smoggy fogs of lung-eating miasma pressed down on the streets, smothering rich and poor alike. Cordelia slapped her hands together and realised that as the alcohol dissipated, she was now cold. She began to walk around, stamping her feet to stay warm. She was dressed for a hot party inside a house, not roaming around outside. Every stone on the ground pressed its pointy way through the soles of her dancing shoes.

But at least she had her hat, gloves and her light cloak, which she had taken from one of the stewards as she left the house. She pulled the cloak around her, and hugged her small bag to her chest.

The remaining few guests were leaving now. She pulled back, almost hiding herself in a glossy-leaved laurel hedge.

Where was Stanley? He had accompanied her, driving a small, one-horse hired carriage, and he should have stayed around until she was ready to leave. Some guests were walking home, in small groups. Others were driving their own light gigs, but not many folks kept their own horses in the city. A few would find a cab to take them home; there were always plenty to be found, day or night.

The yard in front of the house was now empty. She prowled around and looked up at the yellow spots of light in the otherwise black and blank windows. She could hardly re-enter the house, now. She would only embarrass the Duke by being the sole remaining guest. He would not be able to retire, or move on to other entertainments, until she had left.

She paced, sticking to the shadows. She heard a bolt being shot home and the light in the window beside the main door was snuffed out.

She turned and went to the wide entrance that let out onto the street, and looked up and down. There were no coaches or cabs nearby.

There was something much further down the street, though. And the large bulk of a coach or carriage. She could only make out shadowy figures in the gloom; one person standing, and the cab on the street next to them. Even though they were standing under one of the new gas lights, it hardly illuminated anything more than the shape of their body to identify them as human. The person was talking to another who was sitting on the seat of a cab. She was not sure if it was Stanley or not; everything was dark. That far gas light was the nearest one to her, so sparsely spread out were they.

Well, if Stanley is not here, then I must make my own way home, she resolved. She had money and other such things needful in an emergency all secreted in her bag. She wished now for another drink to give her courage and warmth. She set her shoulders and began to walk down the street towards the cab and the two figures.

Her soft shoes made no sound but the figure on the ground looked up. They must have caught her movement. She saw that it was a man, tall, and muffled up against the spring night coldness. He lifted an arm as if he was pointing her way, and then turned away.

He was gone, well out of sight, by the time she reached the cab. It was one of the newer Hansoms, all thin and spindly and light and fast, with one horse, dancing on its feet.

"Are you for hire?" she asked, looking up. It was certainly not Stanley who sat atop.

"I am indeed, mistress. That gentleman there said you might have more need of it than he."

"How thoughtful of him. I would have shared."

"Best not, begging your pardon, mistress, but these times are dangerous ones. Hop in. And where to, if you please?"

"Furnival's Inn."

"Right you are. We'll not be long." He had a pleasant, agreeable voice, gravelly, with a rough tone that reminded her of Geoffrey and that was a calming memory.

He leaped down from his seat at the back and helped her into the cab. The door took two attempts to close, and he took to slamming it very hard. She had to scuttle her feet back out of the way. She settled back into the none-too-plush interior. She was open to the elements from the waist above, though there was a blanket provided for her comfort. It was greasy to the touch, and she resolved not to use it. She gritted her teeth, and hoped that the journey would be quick.

But it was not.

The driver whipped up the horse into a fast trot, it was true; in fact the steed was urged to a much swifter pace than was common. The carriage rocked alarmingly from side to side, the springs creaking and squealing. She hammered on the roof to make him slow down, but he either could not hear her, or did not care to. There was a trapdoor up there, through which she could have poked her head to shout at him, but when she tried it, she found it was stuck firmly closed.

Perhaps he is in a fearful hurry to be home himself, she thought. She clung to the sides and craned her neck, shouting, but he paid her no heed. Thwarted, she nestled back into the centre of the seat, and that was when she realised they were nowhere near the Inns of Chancery.

They were heading to the docks.

CHAPTER TWENTY-SEVEN

She gripped the front edge of the wooden half-doors and peered forwards, as the cold air stung her face and uncurled her hair into medusa locks about her. The horse was so close to her that she could smell its sweat and that warm fogginess particular to the equine species. The noise of its hooves on the varying ground was loud, but the bustle of the night trade around her was equally noisy. They careered past a warehouse that opened on to a wharf, where a ship was being unloaded by the poor light of lanterns and lamps. Men shouted and hollered as they trotted past, and someone threw a soft rag and a warning their way, but the cab rolled on.

Then they turned down a street that was entirely empty and still.

Had the cab driver suffered an attack, and expired?

No, she realised. The whip was lifted and cracked

across the poor animal's rump from time to time, and she heard a cry from above that must have come from the driver.

Was this a robbery? Was she to be taken to a lonely spot, and relieved of her jewels? She fingered the diamond necklace she wore. She would not miss it. They could have her earrings and her brooch, too.

Except that it was the *principle* of the thing, blast it! Now she had an estate and income from her stocks, she had other jewels. That wasn't the point! That some common thief thought he might simply take what was not his — no, it could not be.

There were cases of footpads lingering outside the residences of the rich, and targeting those who left, knowing that there were many fine people with much wealth about their persons, especially when there were parties. Was she one such unlucky person?

Or, she thought, *is this targeted? Are they after me? If so, why?*

Oh — the investigation, she then thought. *Could it be that? If they had wanted to simply rob me, they would have done so by now.*

Therefore, they must have another destiny in mind for me. She shivered. *I have to get away, right now.*

She began to fumble and kick at the half-door by her legs, but it was now wedged shut, and quite immobile. *No matter,* she thought. *I can jump over it.*

The horse's hind legs pumped up and down, in a smart trotting action. The ground seemed to rush beneath her. She leaned out but she could not imagine how she'd be able to fling herself free of the cab, and avoid being crushed by the wheels. She was encumbered by her skirts, her crin-au-lin and her corset, and her soft-soled shoes would be no protection from the landing.

Instead, she would have to wait. She opened her bag and began to feel around inside. Something would be able to help her. She had taken Ruby's advice.

You must be clever, the maid had said.

I am, Cordelia thought. *But am I clever enough?*

***

The cab swung sharply to the left and she slammed into the side, but she didn't let go of the small cloth bag in her hands. It was a pudding cloth. She had dragged it from the depths of her ordinary bag. Now she pulled at the drawstring top, and readied herself; the driver hauled hard on the reins and the horse was brought to a stop.

She did not wait. She scrambled up and over the half-door, holding her skirts up high in her left hand, not caring what might get dirty or torn as she dragged the layers over the side of the cab. She nearly lost her balance, and her feet slipped, but she jumped to the ground and kept hold of her bags — the large one held by the handle in her left hand, the same that was gripping her skirts, and the small drawstring one in her right, ready.

And it was as well that she did.

The cab driver was behind her in an instant, and made to grab her. She felt one hand grip her left arm and she spun around anti-clockwise, to face him, and as she did so, she let the opened drawstring bag fly up and disgorge its contents into his open eyes.

He shouted out some rich and fruity expletives as he fell back, clawing at his face, sneezing and coughing. She did not linger to see what lasting effect the pepper and spices might have on the man. She ran. She dropped the drawstring bag, now empty, shoved her own bag onto her wrist, gathered up her skirts in both hands and ran as hard as she could. She ignored the pain in her feet from the rough ground.

All she could do was run.

Her life depended on it.

She was not going to be the victim of a robbery, a kidnapping or worse. She ran and ran, heading for the noise and bustle of the ships on the wharves that were unloading in the night. Their schedules ran on tides and trades, not light and daytime and sun.

Men shouted at her again, some laughing, some with concern, but she ignored them all. Her lungs hurt and spots danced before her eyes; she was laced up more tightly than usual, and she knew she could not sustain the pace for much longer. She was secretly amazed that she had got further than a few yards.

Her hair was an uncurled, sweaty mess and her bonnet was left far behind. She stumbled, and slowed, and bounced into a wall, her vision clouding as she rasped for breath. She tried to fumble in her bag for another weapon, something else she had pilfered from the kitchens, but her fingers were trembling and did not seem to be able to grasp anything properly. Her skirts were hanging loose again, and only her crin-au-lin prevented them from tangling around her ankles.

"Hold hard, missis, you'll fall into the river," said a young woman's voice close to her ear. "And likely you'll bounce, not drown, such is the filth in it, but it's not such a pretty way to die, even so."

Cordelia stopped. She could not run another step. She sank against the wall, her knees buckling as she fought for air. Her vision was black. Her hearing was clouded by a roaring in her ears.

"Whoa, now! Steady, steady! You had best sit before you fall," the voice said. Warm hands lowered her gently to the ground. She ended up sitting most inelegantly, her legs straight out in front of her, her skirts bowed and billowed up in a heap, and her back ramrod-straight against the wall.

The young woman crouched beside her. She was far less encumbered by any decent clothing. As Cordelia's sight returned to her, she quickly became aware that the woman was mostly dressed for ease of access rather than modesty.

She knew, then, the woman's occupation, and did not need to ask why she was at the dockyards in the dead of night.

"Thank you so much," Cordelia said. "A man was chasing me."

The woman stood up and walked a few yards away, looking and listening. "No one pursues you now. You are quite safe. Well, relatively so."

Was she? Cordelia held her bag tightly and wished she'd had the foresight to take her jewellery off while she was still in the cab. She couldn't do it now, without drawing attention to herself. Her shawl was somewhere in the streets, and her diamonds were on show for anyone to see.

She had to get up, and get home. When she started to her feet, the young woman came to her side instantly, and helped her with an arm around Cordelia's waist.

"My, those are pretty things indeed," she said as the glitter around Cordelia's neck was now obvious. "No wonder you were being chased. Do you take some advice from me, missus, and cover them up with something. Do not put them in your bag," she warned, as Cordelia raised her hand to the clasp at the bag. "For then someone will take your bag, I am sure of it. No, here, take this." She pulled away the loose fringed shawl that she had tied around her waist, and drew it around Cordelia's shoulders. "That will do it."

"Oh. Thank you, again! And might I trouble you for one more favour? Could you tell me where I am? The cab driver brought me here quite against my wishes, you see. It is he that I am running from."

The young woman's face clouded. "It ain't right, not at all, men behaving like that," she said. "I will take you home, missus, because together with me, you will be safer than alone, even if I saw you into a cab. Only..."

Cordelia understood the issue immediately. "I would be very grateful if you were to accompany me home," she said, "and I will pay you for your trouble. You shall not be out of pocket on my account."

The woman smiled. "Thank you, missus. Now, come along with me, and we shall find a cab together."

***

The ride back to Furnival's Inn became a merry one

with the young woman, who revealed her name to be Millie, on board. Millie screeched with laughter when Cordelia introduced herself.

"A real lady?"

"By marriage," Cordelia said.

"As if that do mean anything. You are a lady! Oh my."

"I am not as high born as you might suppose."

"Nah, missus, I can tell you from the way that you just said that very sentence, you are ranks and ranks above me. And here we are, me helping you!"

Cordelia gave her a very shiny guinea, and Millie beamed with delight. "I shall take the rest of the night off," she said as Cordelia alighted from the cab.

Cordelia paid the driver, and slipped him some extra too. "Take the girl wherever she wants," she said, and Millie waved merrily as she departed.

She had no idea what time it was, but she fancied that she could see a lightening in the sky betokening the coming of the morning. It was particularly cold now, especially without a shawl, or the welcome proximity of the happy Millie. She went into her rented rooms as quietly as she could, although a part of her wanted to storm into the men's room and box Stanley's ears for the trouble he had caused her.

She did not dare to think about what had happened to

her, not yet. She knew she had to get inside, lock the door, and feel safe, before she could analyse the events.

The locks were well-maintained and she made little sound as she slipped into the sitting room, and closed the door firmly behind her. It was almost pitch black in the room, but there was a light showing from the kitchen door which was partly open.

In the kitchen she found a candle burning down very low, and Mrs Unsworth slumped in an easy chair that had been put by the range. She was comatose and smelled strongly of alcohol. A gin bottle rolled at her feet and Cordelia knocked it accidentally, causing it to clink and rattle on the stone floor.

It didn't rouse Mrs Unsworth but it was enough to alert Neville Fry, who was in the adjoining room. He had clearly not been sleeping. He flung the door open and stopped and stared when he saw Cordelia.

"My lady!"

"Mr Fry. What is going on here? Why are you awake?" Though she could not be angry with him. She was flooded with relief to see a familiar face. Suddenly, her limbs began to shake and tremble violently.

"I cannot sleep. Is she still...?"

"Yes, she is quite out of her senses," Cordelia said, shaking her head sadly at Mrs Unsworth's slumbering bulk.

"Is Stanley within?" Her knees began to wobble and she tried to sink gracefully onto the bench.

"No, my lady," Mr Fry said, and her blood chilled. "I thought he was with you. And Ruby?"

"No, she is here. Is she not?"

He looked down. "She is not."

"And Geoffrey?" she asked, pleading internally, *let him be here, let him be here.*

"I heard him say he was off to an alehouse, my lady. And he has not returned, but that is not unusual. Ruby and Stanley, however…"

"Oh my goodness. I thank the heavens that you are here, Mr Fry. Please, will you fetch me a drink? The strongest spirits we have in the place, if you will."

"At once, my lady. I shall serve in the sitting room."

"Of course."

He set about his business. She dragged in a breath and forced herself to her feet. She felt she still had to appear strong to her staff. She took a fresh candle and lit it from the spluttering one in the kitchen, and took it through to sit at the table in the sitting room. Neville brought her a glass of brandy with an apology that it was not suitable for ladies, but it was very strong, and that seemed to be the more important matter.

She dismissed him, urging him to go to bed and sleep.

"There is nothing we can do at this hour," she said, trying to sound confident. And it was true. Was she about to suggest they both go careering about the dark London streets? Never. "We must wait until dawn at least."

But once she was alone, she realised that she did not want the drink that Neville had brought for her at all. She watched it for a long while, the candle's dancing light reflecting on the amber liquid. Too much drink had made a fool of her, she knew. It had happened before, too.

Maybe Stanley had a point about abstinence.

She left the glass on the table, paced about the room for a good long while, and eventually took herself to bed.

CHAPTER TWENTY-EIGHT

She had a fitful night's sleep and did not linger in bed once she woke up fully. She estimated that she had slept for only a few hours.

There was still no sign of Ruby.

Cordelia tried not to panic, but fear was flooding her body now. Someone had tried to take her away in a cab, and now two of her staff members were missing. She hastily dressed in a simple day outfit that didn't need much help from a maid, and with hair undone and only loosely laced in, she ran into the kitchen, holding her breath as if that could conjure up her missing staff.

Neville was there, and he shot to attention as she entered.

"No sign of either of them, my lady."

"Then as soon as you have breakfasted, please go out into the streets and do what you can. You must speak to any policemen that you see, and ask at the church, and trace the steps between the Duke's house and here. Spread the word and pay whoever you need to pay."

"At once, my lady." He grabbed a bread roll, and left.

Mrs Unsworth was clearly hungover. She was in a worse state than Cordelia had ever seen before, and Cordelia guessed that she was actually still half-drunk. "I expect you will be wanting a proper breakfast," she said in a surly tone.

Cordelia's stomach clenched. "Something light, please." She sat at the kitchen table.

Mrs Unsworth glowered. It was not often that they were alone together, just the two of them. "It isn't right nor proper that you sit there like that, begging pardon, my lady," she said as she began to saw at a loaf of bread. "I've not even put a white cloth down."

"Well, I shall tell no one, if you shan't," Cordelia said. Ruby and Stanley were missing; who cared about ceremony and standards?

I was nearly kidnapped and taken and … who knows what else, she thought. *I am cross and scared and everything else as well. What do I care for a white table cloth?*

Mrs Unsworth harrumphed and began to beat some eggs, adding in cream and herbs as she set the bowl over some boiling water. The thick slices of bread were laid to toast by being placed in a thick, heavy pan and covered over. The range, being an enclosed one, had no way of toasting before an open flame, but the pan-made toast was just as good, albeit needing to be done with thicker slices which would then be split open.

"Nevertheless, people talk," Mrs Unsworth muttered.

"And where does that talk begin?" Cordelia snapped, irritation close to the surface. She was too stressed to hold her tongue as she would usually do. "You must accept that I am the mistress here, and that my household is an unconventional one. I know that I am talked about, and I know that many would consider my ways radical and even dangerous. Sometimes I wonder why you stay with me."

"You know why I stay."

"You think that you have to? You have no obligations here. You can leave. I would even provide you with a reference."

"I thought that I might, as it happens. I could stay here in London. I'd be closer to Jasper." When she uttered that name, she slammed down the bowl onto the table and drew in a shuddering breath. "I have been to see him."

"I thought that you might, while we are here, and I do not blame you for it."

"Yet I—"

"Blame me?" Cordelia said, her anger rising. She got

to her feet. "There are things you do not know about your son. And what is more, his—"

The door burst open, and two ragged figures almost fell into the room, stopping Cordelia's rising argument dead.

"Ruby! Stanley!"

They were scuffed and dirty and their faces were strained, with dark circles under their eyes. Stanley steered Ruby to the easy chair by the range, and she collapsed into it. The boy then folded himself onto the bench by the kitchen table and slumped forward. Neville Fry followed, having clearly met them out in the streets. He removed himself to the sitting room, probably to find things to polish.

"My lady ... I am sorry ..." Stanley said, trying to stand up again.

"Stanley, stay sitting. Mrs Unsworth, hot drinks, now. No, no, leave the eggs, let them spoil. London eggs start out half-spoiled anyway. Ruby, are you hurt?"

"No, my lady. Just tired."

"And Stanley?"

"I am unhurt."

"What has happened? Shall I send for the police? Or a doctor?"

Stanley shook his head and looked towards Ruby, who waved her hand and closed her eyes, turning her head away. She looked utterly exhausted.

Hesitantly, and with his customary stammer, Stanley began to explain what had happened.

He began with an apology.

"I left the Duke's house. There was nothing for me in the servants' hall; I was in the way. In the stables, there were others playing dice, and again, as you know that is not for me. And the head man there was complaining at the number of people who had brought coaches. He felt it was a rude imposition on his master's hospitality. So I took the hired carriage and went for a walk along peaceful lanes, and came to a church, and went to sit in the porch for a moment of reflection."

"Oh no. And when you left the church…"

"Exactly, my lady, the carriage and horse had gone. I thought I was watching. I closed my eyes only for a minute. And I heard nothing in that minute. But the horse and carriage had gone. It could not have gone far, and I began to run, to find it, but there was no sign!"

"An opportunistic thief," Cordelia said. "And a clever one. Oh, Stanley, you silly innocent."

He hung his head in shame. "So then I came back to the house to find you, but the place was in darkness. I met a tall man outside, and I told him who I was and who I was looking for. He said that he knew you and had been speaking with you, but that you had gone home. And that everyone had gone. I could see that the doorway was unlit, and there was no sign of any staff in the stables either. So then what could I do? I came back here, and expected that you had come home in a cab, as the stranger had said."

"I tried," Cordelia said. "But, please, go on."

"Ruby was here, and she was as frantic as I was when I told her the tale. We both went straight out to find you."

"You didn't think to find Geoffrey, or tell Mrs Unsworth or Mr Fry what was happening?"

"Geoffrey was absent, as was Mr Fry at that moment, and we had no time to wait. As for Mrs Unsworth, well..."

"Already drunk," Cordelia said. Mrs Unsworth didn't say anything. She had made hot drinks and was now preparing a fresh set of eggs and toast for Cordelia.

Stanley nodded miserably. "So out we went, Ruby and I. But things went ill. It was dark and we searched all the streets between here and the Duke's house. A policeman stopped us, as he thought we were suspicious, but he could not help, and ordered us home. We took a back route and then we were set upon."

At this, Ruby opened her eyes and yawned. She said, "We had become separated. He was ahead of me, and I was behind, looking down an alleyway. I heard them before I saw them; two thugs, one threatening to bash Stanley over the head."

"What did you do?"

"I ran up behind them and bashed him first," she said. "The thug, I mean, not Stanley. Then I grabbed Stanley and we ran, but they followed. Thing is, people don't like being smacked on the noggin."

"I am sure that they do not."

"We ran and ran," Stanley said.

"And then we were lost. Even I," Ruby added sadly.

"We had no money for a cab, and we were hungry and thirsty. We walked and walked. I think we must have walked miles in the wrong direction. We eventually had to stop and rest, and we said we'd try to sleep until the sun came up, and we found a space to hide behind boxes near to a market, but they start work early in the mornings and we had no rest at all."

"And here we are now," Ruby said. "And I, for one, am glad to see you safe and sound, my lady."

"I think we have all had adventures," Cordelia said. "But now, you pair must wash and eat and then go to bed. Mrs Unsworth, put the toast and eggs onto two plates for these pair."

"Must I make a third set for yourself?" she muttered.

"You must. See to it."

While they ate, Cordelia told them what had happened to herself. She downplayed it to some extent as she didn't want to alarm them, but there was no nice way of saying "I was taken off in a cab by a footpad." And speaking about it seemed to lessen the shock a little. It was the first time Mrs Unsworth had heard the tale too. Even she looked shocked.

"And you truly believe it was a targeted attack, my lady?" Ruby asked.

"I do, now."

"And ours? Was it linked?"

"That is more complicated. There is the matter of the stolen cab, the man whom Stanley met, and the two thugs who tried to mug you. The man that you spoke to, Stanley, was he well-spoken?"

"He was, my lady. He was elegant and refined. And older gentleman."

"Lord Brookfield, perhaps," she said. "I wonder if he saw me get into that cab? That would explain why he said what he said to you. But as for the stealing of your carriage, Stanley, that sounds opportunistic. There was an unattended horse, and a fine one at that; it was bound to have been stolen."

Stanley hung his head. "It was late and quiet and it caught me out," he said.

"Now, as for the attempted mugging of you both, that is also likely to be chance also."

Stanley said, "You are correct, my lady. I think they simply saw me and saw that I was frantic and unfamiliar with the area, and realised I would be an easy mark. And a foolish one."

"Oh, what an absolute nightmare." Cordelia rubbed at her aching forehead. She had only picked at the food that Mrs Unsworth had set in front of her. She pushed it away.

Mrs Unsworth snatched it away from her. "You are done with this?"

"Mrs Unsworth, have a care to watch your manners. But yes, I am finished. I thank you for the food, but remember your place."

"As we have lately discussed, my lady, perhaps my place is better elsewhere."

"Perhaps it is, though ... though I would counsel you to remember all I have done for you."

Mrs Unsworth scraped the food from the plate, noisily clattering it on the side of a metal bucket. "For me? Yes, putting my son in prison was the least of it."

A silence descended with the heaviness of a body falling to the floor.

No one could quite believe what they had heard.

"Stanley, Ruby, go to bed," Cordelia said. "I will walk out to clear my head."

"Alone?"

"No, I assume that clot Geoffrey is sleeping in a heap somewhere about the place. Stanley, if he is within, kick him awake when you go to your bed."

"Yes, my lady."

CHAPTER TWENTY-NINE

London was a leveller of class. For all the scandal and the gossip, still it would turn a blind eye to certain blatant breaches of propriety. If Cordelia had walked through a county town, accompanied only by her coachman, who was dressed in yesterday's clothes and smelling less than fragrant, she would have been turned away from any reasonable residence; every mistress would have been "not at home" to her calls. She would have endured a well-meaning visit of concern from the local vicar, and no doubt some worthy matrons would have also weighed in with their opinions on her morals.

Here, though, in the steaming pile of humanity that was the greatest city on earth, she was hardly remarked upon. There were far more interesting things to see. She was a minor lady. This was where the Queen herself lived! Every rank of nobility and aristocracy trod the same streets as the lowliest beggar and the least of people.

Granted, there were areas that were closed to certain kinds of people. The very rich areas around Piccadilly were the exclusive haunts of titled folks, and anyone who had less than £1000 a year would have felt out of place there. At the other extreme, though Cordelia had explored some of the poorer areas with the Mission Ladies, even they would fear to tread the very lowest rookeries where the buildings were crowded so close that daylight never penetrated, and sickness lingered in the foetid pools of slurry that stood stagnant on the ground while babies slumped from their dead mothers' arms, already born into addiction and despair.

But the largest part of London was an egalitarian place of noise, because it was a trading city, and money was more important than even one's class. By trade, the nation had grown, and by trade, the Empire had become a thing of wonder. By trade, was one man the master of another not by birth but by work — and money. And money did not care into whose hands it flowed.

She told Geoffrey carefully about the night's events. He agreed with her assessment of the theft of the carriage, and the attempted attack on Stanley and Ruby. "It happens all the time," he said morosely. She was reticent in her description of her own escapades, because she suspected he would react most passionately, and he did. She sought to reassure him that she had never felt in danger.

"Doesn't matter if you felt in danger or if you did not, though, my lady," he said angrily. His pace had quickened as his blood boiled. "Because you *were* in danger, see, and that is that. You must not be alone at any time, do you mark me?"

She chose to overlook his manner in giving her an order. His fury made her feel better. She understood his demands. "And that is why I asked you to accompany me this morning."

"And what is our mission?"

"I needed to walk, and to clear my head."

"In London air?"

"We must find a park," she said. They had walked south of the Inn, towards Fleet Street, but then turned right along The Strand. Many of the finer mansions had been given up as their owners moved west, and there were a great many theatres and entertainments being offered. Cordelia wondered if she was outside society enough to be able to attend the theatre without too much scandal.

As they got closer to Charing Cross and the new hospital, the buildings became modern; great grand edifices in pale London brick, not yet tarnished by the blackening pollution.

And finally, after a little over a mile of walking, they reached the serene sanctity of London's oldest park, St James's.

They had walked in silence, which suited Cordelia. Geoffrey had slowed his pace, and remained alert, looking all around him. He began to walk closer to Cordelia. She stepped aside to give him space but he pressed up against her again, and whispered in her ear without looking at her.

"Do not be in any way alarmed, my lady. But we are being followed. We have taken a random route in this park and yet the same figure is behind us that has been there since we left the lodgings."

She did not let her step falter. She, too, kept her head facing forwards. "Is it one person alone? Have you any idea who they are?"

"They seem small, like a boy not yet a man."

"Oh. Well, I am not scared of that."

"They might not be working alone," Geoffrey said. "Nor might they be unarmed. Do not be scared ... but we must be alert."

"This confirms it," Cordelia said. Geoffrey steered her towards an open section of grass. She was going to get stains on her shoes but she did not care. She let him lead. "That attack on me last night was not a random one, was it?"

"I suspect not, my lady. Hmm, they are flitting from

bush to bush on our right — no, don't look."

"Someone knew I was there, and someone arranged it all to happen, to me and to Stanley," she said. "Why?"

"The murder, of course," Geoffrey said. "You are scaring someone and they want to stop you."

"How awful. How awfully thrilling."

"Let us go up there, and curve around that bush," he said. "We will head to the right but as soon as we are out of sight, you must dart to the left behind the hawthorn."

They strolled as if they did not have a care in the world, but her heart was hammering, ready to make the move on Geoffrey's signal. They wandered around the blowsy-looking hydrangea and Geoffrey touched her arm lightly. She jumped to the left, and hid herself as best she could behind an old and twisting hawthorn tree. It had been cut hard down and had produced many branches and stems from its base, forming a thick shrub.

Whoever was following had assumed they were going to the right, and had chosen to skirt around the right hand side of the hydrangea. Geoffrey leaped out at them, and grabbed them.

They shouted in a high pitched voice but within moments there was a thud and a low growl, and both figures disappeared from view.

Cordelia didn't hesitate. She ran out from her hiding

place and discovered Geoffrey lying on the floor, his black coat spread out and almost covering the smaller figure that was lying squashed beneath him. The boy was struggling like a fish, flapping his hands and feet, and mewling.

"Geoffrey, have a care! You'll hurt him!" she called.

"That's exactly what I'm trying to do," he said, his voice muffled by the flailing limbs.

"Get up! The pair of you, up on your feet, right now."

Geoffrey rolled off the boy but managed to keep a firm grip of him. He twisted the boy's right arm up behind his body, and held the hand at such an angle that any movement the boy made caused him to yell in pain. Geoffrey stood behind the boy and shoved him towards Cordelia. "Do you recognise this little guttersnipe, my lady?"

She peered at the grubby lad closely. He seemed to be around twelve years of age, but with roughened skin and dark bags beneath his eyes. He was underfed and spat expletives at her.

"I do not," she said. "Who are you?"

He began to spout some foul words until Geoffrey shook some civility into him. "Speak well or lose your tongue completely," Geoffrey growled in a low and sinister voice, directly into the boy's ear.

The boy froze.

"Who are you? And why were you following us?"

"I wasn't."

"You were. Who are you?"

"William Lightfoot," he said, with a surly edge only slightly tinged by fear and pain.

"It means nothing to me," she said.

"It wouldn't, would it?"

She thought fleetingly that it was to do with Mrs Unsworth and her son, Jasper, and of course Jasper's wife. "Who sent you?" she asked.

"I dunno. Some rich toff."

Not Mrs Unsworth's doing, this, then. "And his name?"

"I dunno."

But another shaking from Geoffrey tore the name from the boy's mouth. "All right! Mister, hey mister, leave off. It were a cove as was called Hugo Hawke."

"No!" She stepped back and flung her hands up in surprise as if to ward off what the boy was saying. "Why?"

"I dunno. I swear that I do not! Upon my mother's life. If she's alive. Which I doubt."

"Do you believe him, my lady?"

"I do," she said. "He would not have come out with that name under any other circumstances. But it is not at all what I expected to hear."

"And what about the other one?" Geoffrey said.

"What other?" both Cordelia and the boy said at the

same time.

"There was another. I had not spotted him at first. But when I leaped upon this slum-rat, I saw another, a taller one, rush away into the bushes. So this one was not working alone."

"I was, I am, I swear it! There is only me."

Geoffrey shook him and twisted the boy's arm until he screamed and Cordelia ordered him to stop, but he would not confess that he was with someone else.

"Let it drop," Cordelia said. "I think we might get more answers from Mr Hawke himself."

Geoffrey took Cordelia's words literally and the boy was dropped to the ground. He snivelled a moment then was up on his feet, and he swore again, most colourfully and with amusing invention as he ran away.

"I rather think that we have got the wrong one," Cordelia said to Geoffrey, who was looking as pleased with himself as a spaniel that had brought back a game bird.

"We got one of them, my lady."

"No, I suspect that this one was sent to watch me in case I found out anything interesting that Hugo Hawke would want to know," she said. "Annoying but harmless, I think."

"Are you sure?"

"No," she said. "Not entirely. Come, Geoffrey.

Contain yourself for a short while. But I shall unleash you
— and your skills — upon Mr Hugo Hawke as soon as I
may. If it proves necessary," she added. "I may prevail in
my own way. Let us see."

CHAPTER THIRTY

At first, she felt as if she was, indeed, prevailing. Hugo let them both into his receiving room. He looked with distaste at Geoffrey, and the coachman stared him right back as if he were an equal. Cordelia flicked her fingers at Geoffrey and he sulkily went to stand by the door, like a footman awaiting orders. But he half-leaned, and made every effort to look as un-servant-like as possible.

Hugo confessed immediately, and tried to make his actions sound perfectly natural. "Yes, my dear Cordelia, of course I was having you followed! It was simply to ensure that if, by some chance, you forgot to tell me something important, I would know it anyway. It was saving you trouble, you know. I was actually doing you a favour."

"By having me kidnapped in a cab and taken to the docks?"

He laughed in a short, sharp way but it died when he

saw that she was not joking. He looked from her to Geoffrey and back again, disbelief plain on his face. "What?" he said, his shock making him rude. "What do you mean by that? What has happened?"

"What, exactly, were your orders to the boys following me?"

"Boys, plural? There was only ever one. Will something-or-other. And all that I asked him to do was to follow you, and report back to me. Stupid clot. I should have followed you myself." He frowned. "What kidnap? You must tell me, what happened?"

"Goodness, Hugo, you almost sound concerned."

"I am, as it happens. You are the most infuriating woman and a double-crosser, too, but even so, credit me with a modicum of human sympathy. Although it is misplaced if I have any such feelings for you, of course."

But he did look concerned and it softened her. She said, "Well, in short, I was taken off in a cab by some hoodlum but I managed to escape. I have no idea by whom this was orchestrated, or what their ultimate purpose was. Also, my boy Stanley encountered an issue and was misdirected by persons unknown; that, however, might have been an innocent mistake."

Hugo went to a drinks cabinet. "Cordelia, I am sorry for it all. I hope you were not hurt. Would you care for something to sooth your nerves?"

She remembered her indiscretions while inebriated. "No, thank you. So, you are quite sure that you have no knowledge whatsoever about this incident?"

"None at all," he said, pouring himself a small glass of whisky and adding a little water. "I hope you know that it would be quite beneath me. Tell me, who else have you annoyed lately, aside from me? Oh, and how did that little meeting with Socks go? I am still awaiting my thanks for arranging that, you know. I let you in today only because I was expecting plaudits not accusations."

She almost smiled at how quickly his words turned from sympathy to his habitual mocking of her. She almost felt a warmth of familiarity.

"I have my suspicions of him, yet," she said. "I need to discover exactly where he was on the night of the murder. As for anyone else, I do not think I have annoyed anyone."

"You are blushing, Cordelia."

"I am not," she said furiously, feeling the heat rise in her cheeks."

"Go on. You have spoken with others."

"Many others. I was at a ball last night. Oh, well, if you must press me so: there was the delightful Lord Brookfield, who, alas, did not catch me at my best last night. However, I hardly think my distracted manner would have been enough for him to wish to kidnap me."

"Lord Brookfield? Ha, well, he and Socks are as thick as thieves, that pair, so if you suspect one you must suspect the other."

She froze. Neither man would admit to knowing the other in any great depth.

Yet from the outside, other people had suggested they were friends.

Hugo's words simply confirmed that impression.

"Both of them deny knowing the other," she said quietly.

"Well," he said, almost jovially, "you cannot claim Lord Brookfield as a murderer. That would be the end of everything, you know."

CHAPTER THIRTY-ONE

"And why can I not?" Cordelia demanded. "Listen. I am tired, I am slightly hungover, and I am frustrated by everyone's lies. Your own, included!"

Hugo pulled out a chair for her, but she remained standing. He shrugged and flung himself into a chair of his own, and thrust out his long legs before him, lying back, with the half-drunk glass of whisky dangling from one hand. "It's simply the way of the world, Cordelia. You can go after Albert Socks because he's nobody, really. But the Lord Brookfield? Well, you've met the man. He's somebody. He's untouchable. You might as well try to call out the Right Honourable Sir Robert Peel and have him brought up for treason or some such. You just can't."

"But if he is guilty…"

"That's for the magistrates, though, is it not? And it hardly matters how decent and upstanding a new one might be."

She stopped, and stared at Hugo. "What did you say?"

"I said, you cannot pin anything on Lord Brookfield."

"No, I mean about the magistrate. He's new, is he?"

"Yes, well, as it happens, there is a new one in my area. Although I suppose that where the crime was committed, the man won't have any influence there anyway. I am finding that frustrating."

Cordelia was desperately trying to keep it all straight in her head. She remembered her talks with Ivy. "There are two magistrates in Holborn division," she said, "and one is ill."

"My, you are well-informed," he said.

"So to which magistrate do you refer?"

"Neither of them; forgive me, I was speaking of another matter entirely."

She watched his face carefully. He'd slipped up about something, she could see that. "You are referring to your own situation, are you not? And what is bad, for you, about a new and decent magistrate in your division? I am still unclear as to your situation."

"More whisky," he said brusquely, and held out his glass.

Geoffrey growled. But Cordelia held herself with dignity, took his glass, and went to pour him another. She did not hand it back. She held it, standing a few feet in front of him, and swirled the glowing golden liquid around. He watched it hungrily.

"You're waiting for me to tell you, aren't you?" he said. "I should snatch that from your hands."

"But you won't," she said. "Now, speak, for I am tired of your games and I am very close to throwing this in your face — glass and all."

He lifted his lip in a snarl, but he remained seated and his body language was that of resignation and defeat. "I can see no reason to keep it secret," he said, "although it paints me in a bad light, I am sure. However you probably expect that already."

"I am not your judge," she reminded him.

"But you will judge me, won't you?" he said, bitterly. "I know how I seem to you, even now. Well, then. The previous magistrate in the division where I have my public house was a friend of mine. We had an understanding. He would allow me to install a publican of my choice, and he would issue the licence for the sale of alcohol."

"I see."

"Do you? I don't think so. The old magistrate understood how business works. He knew that my public house offered certain entertainments to the working man, and that was accepted. But this new one, well, he's not at all happy about how things ought to be run. He's altogether too upright and moral about the whole thing. And you see, the police are so dashed corrupt that they can use this man's blind righteousness. They are threatening me with exposure to him unless I pay them. I have tried to seek help at Bow Street because of their jurisdiction over the others, but I have got nowhere. I am the victim here, but no one seems to have any sympathy at all."

She rolled her eyes, and passed him his drink. "You are right," she said. "I have no sympathy for you and your plight. I assume, therefore, you can't simply go to the magistrate and tell him that the police are blackmailing you?"

"Of course not! For then he would want to know why. Yes, he would have some of the policemen dismissed — why, dozens are being sacked on a weekly basis, anyway — but he would also close my public house. I cannot risk it."

It made his actions seem a little more understandable now. She still thought he was quite mad, but he was obviously at a loss for what to do. He was clutching at straws, and she was the straw. She felt a little sorry for him.

"Perhaps I can talk to the magistrate, subtly...?"

He laughed, and shook his head. "No. No, I shall do this in my own way. I need that magistrate out of office, somehow. Mostly, I need the police to be exposed, but with no links to my own work and practises. And I need more

270

boxing to happen in my pub, so that I have more drinkers, and more betting. And hence, more money."

A plan was beginning to form in Cordelia's mind. "Hugo, these boxers ..."

"What of them?"

"They are rough, strong, violent men, I suppose."

"Of course. What are you planning?"

She ignored his question and half-turned to address Geoffrey, who had been listening with an increasingly amused look on his grizzled face. "I shall need to speak to Florence Fry once more," she said. "And also Ivy Delaney, of course. Come, Geoffrey. I need to get back to Furnival's Inn, get changed, and begin my visits. I shall collect Ruby, also."

"I will accompany you, my lady," he said, opening the door to let her out. "You may still be followed."

"Not by me or mine!" Hugo called after them, his voice seeming small and pathetic now.

She did not even speak to say goodbye. She had had enough of his silly plots, and she had plotting of her own to do.

CHAPTER THIRTY-TWO

"We need a proper carriage for the day, not a horrid little Hansom," Cordelia said to Geoffrey.

"At last," he said. "I do agree. Although driving through these streets is a difficult task."

"Nevertheless," she said, "I shall go back to Furnival's Inn, and change, and get Ruby to accompany me while you see to it. We will then ride to Ivy Delaney's house. Oh, I should send her a note to prepare her to come with us."

"You are kidnapping her, my lady?"

"It is not to be joked about. Come! We have a very busy day ahead of us."

"Do we? Oh. Yes, of course, my lady."

She shot a sideways glance at him. Was he smiling? Certainly his stubble seemed to be twitching upwards.

***

Ivy was ready for her. Cordelia had barely alighted from the hired carriage when she saw her friend was already leaving her house and coming down the steps onto the street.

"I was watching for you from the drawing room!" she said. "Isn't this most perfectly thrilling? Oh! And this is...?"

Geoffrey was holding the door open to the carriage and Ivy was halfway in when she spotted Ruby.

It wasn't usual to introduce a servant to a lady of quality. Still, Cordelia adapted the usual rules of introduction. "Ruby, this is Mrs Ivy Delaney. Ivy, this is my maid and she can be trusted utterly."

"Can I?" Ruby said, cheekily.

"In all matters except those of expected behaviour," Cordelia muttered. "Do not push it. Move over, Ruby. I shall sit next to you, and Ivy can have the other seat to herself. Do you travel with your back to the horse, or facing, Ivy?"

"It matters not to me." Ivy slid onto the seat and gathered her skirts to herself, smoothing them down as the door was slammed. "So, Ruby, you are quite the confidante of our good lady, I understand."

Ivy was being so wonderfully attentive, just as if Ruby were another normal person of the same status, that Ruby actually blushed furiously and Cordelia laughed to see it.

She deflected the unwanted attention from her suddenly-awkward maid, and turned Ivy to other conversation by asking her about the current debates regarding the slums and rookeries of London and how they ought to be improved. Ivy seized on the subject and it kept them quite occupied until they reached their destination.

It took some time, but finally they were there.

They were once more at Bow Street Police station house.

***

"Mrs Delaney!" The constable in the lobby was shocked to see her, and his eyes widened as he took in her company — Cordelia, and her maid.

"Ahh, Robert. And how is your wife since the birth of your ... son, wasn't it?"

"She is doing tolerably well, now, madam, since your kind gifts."

"It was nothing, nothing. Tell her she must drink a pint of stout every morning for as long as she is nursing. It will do her the world of good. And let her stay off her feet if you can. Yes, you must take a turn about the house! I am sure you can handle a broom."

"Yes, madam. Of course, madam. Er, your husband..."

"Oh, he is not here. I know that. He will be sitting in court, rattling through cases and thinking of his dinner. No, we are here to pop in on that poor girl in your cells, that sad Miss Fry. Lead on, Robert."

"But madam..."

"Oh, yes, you cannot leave your post here. Quite right." Ivy looked around. They were surrounded by many people, police and ordinary folk alike, and some were staring while others pretended that they were not. "You there, yes, you with the beard. You can stand here for a moment while we go down to the cells?" She didn't even wait for an answer. The moment that the bearded policeman made one step towards them, she patted the one she'd called Robert on the arm. "Marvellous. Lead on, then. Come along, Cordelia, Ruby."

Cordelia resisted the urge to stick her tongue out at the policemen as they wafted past on their way to the cells.

Her good humour was immediately repressed as they descended into the chilly gloom where the prisoners were engaged in what seemed to be continual noise and rioting. Florence was in her customary cell at the end, still alone, and she was looking very ill indeed.

It didn't take long for them to gain access to the cell. Ruby looked around in horror, but Cordelia's attention was fixed on the pathetic figure before them. She had lost a great deal of weight, and her skin was grey and dry. She had acquired a cough, and Cordelia wanted to enfold her in her arms, and feed her soup.

Florence, however, was spiky and aggressive. "Well, you're doing a fine job of getting me out of here," she said sarcastically, before Cordelia had even introduced Ivy.

"This is the wife of the magistrate here," she said. "Mrs Ivy Delaney."

Florence shrugged. "That ain't nothing to me." She briefly remembered her manners and bopped out a perfunctory curtsey. "It ain't her man that I'll be up before, is it? It will be some judge at the big place."

"No, that is true. Yet I am still hopeful that you shan't be up before anyone."

"You have come here to take me home, then?"

"Sadly, no, not yet. But I have some more questions that it is imperative that you answer with complete honesty."

"Go on, then." Florence flung herself onto her low nest of bedding and blankets, and wrapped herself in her arms. "Ask away."

"You said that Albert Socks gave you the key to the room you used at Mrs Clancey's. Is that correct?"

"Yeah. I told you the truth then and I am telling you it now."

"Good. More importantly, Florence, where is that key now?"

Florence picked at her flaking lips. "Well, the police

have it. They took everything I owned to go over and read and look at. Not that I owned much, but there you are. They got it."

"I see. And what else might the police have which could incriminate you?"

"You what?" Florence said, blinking up at them with dull eyes.

"Did you have anything that showed you might be a murderer?" Cordelia said.

"Oh, like, I had a box of knives or a bottle of poison just lying around?" She snorted. "No, course not. I had a few notes, some letters, between Louis and me. That's all. And they just show my innocence. They just show how much we were in love."

Ruby sidled up to Cordelia and whispered, "Just what on earth did he see in her?"

Cordelia elbowed her maid. They were not seeing Florence at her best, and the days — weeks, even — that she had been incarcerated here had not been kind. Who would still be bright, and lively, and free from bitterness? Cordelia knew that she would not be.

"Florence, I now must ask you this. How did you and Louis Bonneville first meet one another?"

Florence half-closed her eyes, and she smiled to herself as she began her recollection. "I was walking in Hyde Park," she said. "I was with another girl from the household, and it was a Monday afternoon, and all of a sudden Mr Socks had come to me and told me to have the afternoon off."

"Time off?" Cordelia said in surprise. "Did he usually do that?"

"Not often, no," she replied. "He told me to go walking. He said there wasn't enough colour in my cheeks. I said, where, and he suggested a park. So I went, and I took Clarissa along with me."

"And did Clarissa have permission to be out?"

"I don't know, nah, I don't think so, but anyway she came. His staff were a bit lax. And as we walked, he … Louis! … came up to us and asked if one of us had dropped a glove. We hadn't. But he kept on walking and talking with us, and that is how it started."

"He asked if you had dropped a glove? Were you not wearing any?"

"We were. But that is what he said. 'Miss Fry, have you lost this?' I will remember it until I die."

That brought Cordelia up short. "Florence! Is that exactly what he said?"

"Yes, I told you, I ain't a liar."

"How did he know your name?"

Florence still had half-shut eyes. "I dunno, but it shows it was true love, don't it?"

"Absolutely not. It shows that it was a set-up, right from the start."

Florence's eyes flew open. "But why?"

"Why, indeed. I have no idea."

"No," Florence said. "He had seen me, and he must have asked around, because it was love at first sight, and that is all."

"It cannot be."

"And why are you so dried up and alone that you think that no one else could ever feel love?" Florence spat out. Ruby took a step forward at this slight towards her mistress, but Cordelia pulled her back.

"I understand that you feel quite lost and alone," Cordelia said mildly, "and that will make you say things that you do not mean."

"I do mean it," Florence said, but she looked away.

Ivy Delaney had been watching and listening with interest. She said, "You know, this really does baffle me, and it has done right from the beginning. Who really wanted this Bonneville chap dead? That is the crux of it. I cannot see why this waif here would want to kill him. So who did?"

Florence pulled at a hangnail on the side of her thumb and Cordelia was transfixed. Her own fingers twitched in painful sympathy. Florence picked at the loose skin, and said, muttering, "Well, it's all of them, all of those dashed politicians, every one of them, sons of dogs that they are. Not one of them wanted change, did they? He were too different to them. He were too modern. They would all want him out of the way. They would all want him dead."

Cordelia's mouth went dry.

Something had slotted into place.

CHAPTER THIRTY-THREE

Gibbs had invited her to his own house, to attend a small, selective dinner party that evening. He had hired in enough staff to make it an occasion, and most of the food was brought in from a nearby eating house, although he had also employed a male cook to create some elaborate sugarwork on the premises — such things would not survive being carried through the streets, unlike a solid, well-made pie.

It was a bohemian crowd, and Cordelia felt more at ease with the dozen or so people than she had in any other social gathering so far. She was able to relax, and no one challenged her about her now-defunct column, or widowed status, or unconventional lifestyle. Indeed, one of the first topics of conversation concerned the political writer Harriet Martineau. Gibbs revealed that he knew the unique woman and assured everyone she was now quite recovered from her long illness. "I had invited her this evening," he said, "but she is embarking on a tour of Palestine and other places, and wrote me a sweet little note begging my forgiveness that she could not attend tonight."

There was a general murmur of disappointment, particularly from Cordelia, as Miss Martineau had long been a literary idol of hers; indeed, Miss Martineau made her living by her pen, and wrote in unconventional subjects.

One man at the table, however, was less impressed than the others with Miss Martineau and her exploits. "She's a Whig, and you know me, Septimus, I live and let live, but she cannot write independently about political matters if she cleaves to one side or another."

"What nonsense!" a slender, heavily wrinkled woman called out. "All the political writers come from one side of the House or another. I don't believe any are truly impartial, and why should they be?"

"How can they make a fair and accurate judgement of what they write?" the man shot back. "We are too ruled by passion these days."

"For it is passion that changes the world!"

"Does the world need changing?" the man asked. He looked wealthy and well-fed. *No*, thought Cordelia. *For you, the world is perfect.*

"Many on both sides think that the world must

change," Cordelia said, seizing her chance. "What about poor late Mr Bonneville? Who was he, really? He had passions, did he not?"

The man snorted, but another man, the husband of the wrinkled woman, nodded. "He is a sad loss indeed. Now, there was a man with true passion, as you say. He was a man who insisted that the world must change. I met him a few times. You know, sometimes I wondered how far he would go, but there was no doubting his sincerity of belief."

"He was full of fire but very little sense," his wife put in.

"He was dangerous, then," Cordelia suggested.

"Oh yes," the others agreed. "To both sides of the House," the wrinkled woman's husband said. "He was a thorn in Peel's side. He urged him on, to do more, to repeal those Corn Laws and open up trade, thus destroying Britain's security. Peel already inclines to such nonsense; he needs holding back, not encouraging. I am sure that he means well, but the end results will be disastrous."

"He was not fully of British stock, was he, that Bonneville?" another person said. "I never met him, but I did hear that one of his grandparents owned much land in the West Indies, and ... well, let us suggest that his flashing dark eyes were not Celtic in origin."

"Though his sympathies lay with the Irish," the

wrinkled woman said. "Did he not support the Maynooth Grant, and we all know how that has ended..."

"Exactly what I am implying. His, ah, uncertain heritage, led his sympathies to fall a little beyond what one would expect from a righteously-born Englishman, if you get my drift. And I certainly don't want to speak ill of the dead, but I suspect they will have an easier time in Parliament now."

"No!" the loudest man barked. "Peel is done for, regardless. You mark my words. He'll be gone by the end of this year."

"And who will be prime minister then?" Cordelia said. "Who is the favourite contender?"

There was some speculation but no one could really say. *It is all rumour and hearsay,* she thought. But there were kernels of truth within it all.

"There's another man who intrigues me," she said, "as it seems to me that political talk is acceptable here."

"Go on," the loud man said. "Septimus does not mind, do you, old boy?"

"As long as we remain civil and friendly."

"Brandy helps," the man said.

Cordelia smiled. "Well, I met this man, one Lord Brookfield. He's a Tory too, is he not?"

"Oh, yes, but he's thoroughly establishment."

"Not a reformer at all? No revolutionary ferment within his breast?"

"Only in the sense that a revolution — a complete revolution of a wheel — returns to one's starting point."

She took that to mean that he wanted society to return to the "good old days" and that was exactly the impression she had had of him.

"And there is another politician I have met," she said, emboldened by the responses so far. "Does anyone know of a Mr Albert Socks?"

Most people shook their heads. The wrinkled woman said, "Should we? Is he an up-and-coming young man?"

Another man laughed. He was quite corpulent and had "potential gout sufferer" written all over his purple and red face. "Up-and-coming, old Socks? Been-and-gone, more like. He likes his games and his cards, but he thinks he is more than he actually is. We all thought he'd be someone, once, when he arrived on the scene and that Lord Brookfield took him under his wing, but he's come to naught, alas, and they have fallen out."

"Oh no," a woman said. "For I did hear that Socks and Lord Brookfield were seen together a few nights ago in Hyde Park, and goodness only knows what they did there, for is it not a place that—"

"Hush, Gertrude! However liberal our dear host is, I

am sure that none of us want to hear quite such scurrilous and unfounded gossip. You think you are still living in the court of the Prince Regent."

"They were fun times," the woman said, but she subsided.

"I asked the Lord Brookfield for recommendations while I stayed here in London," Cordelia said. "You know, where to go and who to see. But he said he did not care for concerts or galleries. So where does he go? Soirees, parties and balls?"

"He is a reluctant attender," the woman told her.

A man put in, "Well, he keeps himself to himself at his club most of the time."

"Which one?"

"He's a Tory; White's, of course, on St James's Street."

"And Socks?"

"I doubt they'd admit that one, even if he asked! I suspect he frequents the usual common places."

"Again," said Gibbs, "let us keep the talk as gentile as we might. Has anyone heard Mr Darwin lecture lately?"

The talk turned to the daring topic of animals and their reproductive habits, shocking a whole new section of the gathering. Cordelia half-listened, but she was glad when the women could retire. After they re-joined the men, she thanked Septimus but made her excuses for an early night.

He led her to his lobby while his staff brought her outdoor clothing, and another footman went to seek out Geoffrey and Stanley who were waiting in a nearby alehouse to chaperone her home. He pressed her hand briefly, and she remembered the heartfelt hug he'd given her before. It was not something he could repeat here, in view of his staff and his guests.

"You were digging for information relevant to your investigation, weren't you?" he said as he helped her into her cloak.

"Of course I was."

"And you stayed sober, and were remarkably subtle. Well done."

"Thank you," she said. "I believe I am learning."

"You certainly are. Ahh, here are your men. They are like bodyguards."

She laughed, but had a feeling of unease. Septimus had no notion of the kidnapping attempt, and she had no intention of telling him. Even now, it seemed like a distant memory, because she had kept her mind busy with other things. No doubt it would return to her in her nightmares in the future, but for now, she had other things to do. She secured her bonnet and pulled on her gloves, and allowed herself to be ushered out into the night.

"Are we still being watched?" she asked Geoffrey.

The streets at night were his natural habitat. He moved in the shadows with the ease of a horse doing dressage. "It is impossible to say, my lady, until they make a move," he said. "And when they do, have no fear. We shall handle them."

She glanced at Stanley, who was quivering slightly.

"Let us hurry home," she said.

CHAPTER THIRTY-FOUR

Mrs Unsworth was in the kitchen when they arrived back at Furnival's Inn. She was slumped in the easy chair, a bottle of gin clutched in her arms. Her eyes flickered as Cordelia entered.

"Where's Ruby?"

"Preparing your bed, my lady," Mrs Unsworth said in a slurred tone.

Cordelia took the half-empty bottle from her arms. Mrs Unsworth clawed at it, but she could not focus with any accuracy. Cordelia placed the bottle on the table, and regarded her drunken cook.

"You have become far worse since we got here. London is bad for you."

"You'd know all about that," Mrs Unsworth said.

"I don't know what you mean," Cordelia replied.

Geoffrey growled but Cordelia waved him down.

"Leave it. She is too far out of her senses to know what she is saying. Ah! Ruby. Come, sit with me. You can all help me work out the next move we must make."

Cordelia pulled the wooden bench away from the table. Ruby looked towards Mrs Unsworth, staring hard at the cook who turned her head away. She was not going to give up her comfortable seat unless directly challenged, and Cordelia had other matters more pressing.

Geoffrey went to a cupboard and helped himself to some bread, taking advantage of Mrs Unsworth's state. He remained in the room, lingering by the warm range, opposite to where Mrs Unsworth sat.

"Now, Ruby, I need to get into Albert Socks' house."

"But why?"

"I need to find evidence."

"What evidence? Pardon me, my lady, but if you blunder in there without knowing what you are looking for, everything might seem like a clue but you will miss the obvious things."

"I do know what I seek, as it happens," Cordelia said smugly. "There were two keys to that room at Mrs Clancey's. Florence had one, and now that is in the possession of the police. The other is with Albert Socks. So I need to procure that key and prove that it is the same as the one that the police have." *And also the same as all the others on that floor of the lodging house,* she reminded herself. *I hope that won't be a problem in court.*

She knew that it could be.

Ruby shook her head, laughing in disbelief. "Really? We are to go into his house and find a key? What, do we knock upon the door?"

"Of course not, silly girl. You yourself told me that his staff are very lax. We will sneak in. I am sure that in the dead of night we might evade any notice, especially as Socks himself is unlikely to be home. I know, now, that he is often at low dives around the city."

There was a strange burbling from the chair by the range. Cordelia saw that Mrs Unsworth was actually laughing.

"You? You two? You two seek to break into a man's house, do you? Ha! Ha! That is hilarious. Who needs gin when I can listen to that!"

"Mrs Unsworth, may I remind you to whom you are speaking," Cordelia said in her most lofty Mistress Voice.

The cook wiped the smile from her face but she appeared in no way contrite. She muttered, "No, you two? Ha. You need a professional for that sort of thing."

"And you'd know one?" Cordelia said.

There was a moment of silence.

"I am serious," Cordelia insisted.

The silence lengthened.

Mrs Unsworth turned and stared at the range. She worked her lips and mouth, as if chewing her cheek on the inside.

"Yeah, well, all right," she said at last. "When I went to see my Jasper, I met all sorts. I took him food, you know. And money, though he seemed to be doing all right for himself, even though it is prison and all."

Ruby was staring at Mrs Unsworth, her eyes wide. Geoffrey pretended not to be listening but Cordelia knew that he was.

"And did you meet anyone ... professional?" Cordelia said in a light tone.

"There were some as might be helpful in this case," she said. "I suppose I might make some enquiries for you."

"Please," Cordelia said. "I am not afraid to beg this of you. Any help you might give would be very, very welcome. I shall be in your debt."

Mrs Unsworth twisted into a nasty smile and looked Cordelia straight in the eye. She nodded towards the bottle of gin. "Aye," she said, gruffly. "That you shall, right enough. That you shall."

CHAPTER THIRTY-FIVE

"This cloak is perfect!" Cordelia said as she wrapped herself in the dark woollen depths. "I told you I needed a proper sleuthing cloak."

"Very good, my lady," Ruby said, shooting a look towards Stanley.

Stanley, however, was in no mood for banter. He was hunched over, his face pale in the gloom of a dark back street near to Albert Socks' house.

Cordelia thought that she ought to have told him to stay at home but he seemed compelled to come with them. She noticed that he hovered near to Ruby, though whether it was for her protection or his own, she could not guess.

Geoffrey clinked and clanked as he moved. She could only imagine what weapons he had ranked about his person, hidden in the depths of his layers. She herself had a fresh batch of black pepper tied up in a pudding cloth, as it was her new favourite means of defence after the successful defeat of the cab driver in the docks.

There was one other in their little group.

Mrs Unsworth had refused to come with them. She had sent, however, a man that she had been able to contact through various disreputable means, and he was standing before Cordelia now, with a broad grin in his gap-toothed face.

He was a few inches shorter than she was, and wiry with gangling arms like a monkey. He was called Dodson — that was all the name they'd been given and she didn't like to ask for more — and he hadn't stopped chortling with delight since she'd met him.

He rubbed his hands together with the glee of a miser in a bank. "Now then, Mrs C," he said, "or milady or whatever, this is my patch now, you see, and my world, so I do ask you all one thing. You must follow along with me and you must all do just what I say, and when I say it, and that way we might all stay safe. Do you agree?"

"Of course, Dodson," she said. She wasn't going to argue about the conventions of address when she was about to ask him to break into someone else's house for her.

"Now then, my friends, this is the first thing: you cannot all come with me, for I won't be having a herd of elephants following along behind and causing a ruckus. It shall be me and you alone, Mrs C."

"No," said Ruby, and Geoffrey swore with much the same meaning.

"That is how it is, I am afraid, my lovelies." Dodson spread his hands wide, his fingers like dark spiders in the night. "You all have some important jobs to do, anyway. I shall place you all around the house, at points up and down the road. We know he has gone out, but we don't know when he might return. At the first sign of him you must run and alert us. Throw dirt against the window."

"Which window?" Geoffrey said crossly, looking up at the four-storey building with its double frontage.

Ruby sighed dramatically. "All of them along the first floor," she said.

"Why do you think that?"

"Well, they are going to go to his study, don't you think? If I were a man keeping a key it would be in my own study. The top floor is for the servants. The ground floor is for visitors. And the third floor will be bedrooms."

"You're clever," said Dodson. "You had better stay out here, with the best view up and down the main street. You, boy, before you wet yourself, off you go and stand at the far end of this street. You sir," he said to Geoffrey, "I would recommend you go up the other end. It is more likely that he returns that way, from town. Do what you must to delay him, and this lively girl here will notice, and throw up the dirt to alert us. Is that most clear?"

"It is," said Cordelia, impressed. "Let us wait no longer. Dodson, please, lead on."

"Right you are, Mrs C. Follow me, and step as light as you can."

Cordelia was nearly sick with excitement. Somehow, in the company of her staff and in particular the confident and oddly charming Dodson, she felt like it was all a silly adventure.

That was, until they crept to the front door. There were steps to the right that led down to the area in front of the house, fenced off from the street by iron railings. Dodson led her that way, creeping into the inky blackness where he began to prise at a small window.

She could not see what he did but suddenly the pane of glass fell forwards silently into his waiting hands. He laid it carefully on the floor.

"Prized out the putty, Mrs C," he said cheerfully when he saw her peering at it. "Come along now, and silently."

He slithered through the window, and Cordelia stared at the opening.

There was no way her dresses would fit through that.

Dodson poked his head back out. "Are you coming?"

"I can't." She gestured hopelessly at her wide hips.

He rolled his eyes but there was a good-humoured smile on his face. "Go up to the door then, as soon as I open it."

She waited in the shadows until she heard the faint creak of the front door opening from inside, and she darted up the steps. He pressed it closed behind her and led her quickly through the hall. Nothing was lit, save one lamp to light Socks' way on his return. She strained her ears and caught very distant laughter.

"The servants in the hall beyond," Dodson whispered as he crept up the stairs, testing each tread for a squeak before he committed his full weight to the step. "And if we can hear them from here, I would wager they are making very merry with the master's alcohol."

From what Cordelia knew of them, that sounded very likely.

Now it felt less like a game, and more like dangerous folly. Actually being inside the house, so close to the other occupants, made Cordelia realise that this wasn't a fun little adventure.

She could be arrested once again, and this time there would be no chance of bail.

Now they were on the first floor landing. There was one lamp lit, at the far end, where another set of stairs snaked upwards. Dodson pressed himself far too close to

Cordelia, and whispered, "Any idea which one is the study?"

"Not a clue," she hissed back.

Dodson then went to each door in turn, silently padding along in his soft-soled shoes, and sniffed at each door, bending to put his nose close to the keyholes.

"This one!" he said suddenly, raising his hand.

"How can you tell?" she asked as she dashed to his side.

"It smells more strongly than any of the others of pipe tobacco," he explained. He twisted the handle. "And luck is on our side, Mrs C. It ain't locked." He tutted. "You think these rich folk would have more sense. Anyone might come along. People like us!"

"Indeed," she said.

He opened the door very slowly and steadily. She knew why he had to move so carefully but it made her feel tense. Her palms sweated and her scalp felt prickly and itchy. He slid through a narrow gap and she followed, opening the door a little wider to accommodate her skirts.

The cloak was all very well, but she perhaps should have dressed a little more for house-breaking than house-calls.

She was impressed by Dodson's guesswork and strategy. They were, indeed, in the study. Dodson went to the windows and looked out. "We are by the street," he said

300

in a low voice. "I can see your girl down there. She's a bold one. Does she have a sweetheart?"

Cordelia glared at him but he had his back to her. "Yes," she hissed. "Many."

He sighed in disappointment. "Right, to our task! This key. Have you any idea what might distinguish it from any other key?"

"I suspect that it will be on its own, not part of a bunch or set. It will be unmarked, or have the name of a lodging house — Mrs Clancey's — on it. It will be plain, and much used, as it is one given out to those who rent a room in this particular place."

"That helps," he said. "And will he not miss the key?"

"I do not intend to take it," she said. "For that will mark me as a thief and I've already had one brush with the law. I do not want to give them more ammunition against me."

"Then what will you do with this key?"

She smiled, and he was facing her now. "Wait and see."

They got down to the task. There was a gas lamp in the street outside but it barely illuminated two feet around it, and lent very little light to the room itself. But their eyes had adjusted to the gloom, and Dodson had brought a stub of a candle which he lit and shaded with his hand.

She worked methodically. She went first to his desk

and began to open drawers. She soon hit upon one that was locked, and Dodson stepped in. He crouched down and inserted a fine length of wire. Curiously, he turned his head away, and closed his eyes. He appeared to be listening intently to the lock mechanism as he made tiny movements of his fingers.

And then the drawer sprang open and he stood up with an even wider grin than normal. "I do get an uncommon sense of achievement in my line of work, Mrs C," he said. "I'd recommend this as a change of job for anyone who feels a little jaded, you know."

"Goodness. I will bear it in mind."

She peered into the drawer. There was a bundle of paperwork tied up with a ribbon and she studied it to see if it offered any clues. Sadly it didn't have a signed confession on it; it seemed to be business relating to voting and policies and something to do with the current state of famine in Ireland. The writing was in black but another hand had scrawled across the top, in red, "Fifteenth of May!" The dots over the letter "i" were formed with circles, like a child would do. She wondered what was to happen in the following month. She put the documents aside and looked towards the back of the drawer.

"I have it!" she said suddenly.

"Hush!" Dodson came to her side and looked at the

key. "May I?"

"For a moment." She handed it to him and fished around in a pocket that she had tied on around her waist before she'd left her own lodgings. She brought out a small piece of biscuit dough that she had carefully wrapped in waxed paper, and laid it on the desk.

After staring at the key intently, Dodson handed it back to her, and she pressed it into the dough. "I have worked on this for days," she said. "I wanted to find a mixture that would hold a shape most accurately, and this is it."

"That is clever, indeed," Dodson said. "But I ought to tell you that as soon as we leave this place, I could draw out the key in its exact shape and take that image to a locksmith who would make up an exact copy, you know."

"Your powers of recall are strong."

"Not so; it is a trick," he said. "See here." He held the key up horizontally between them so that it was more visible in the darkness. "You must imagine a set of lines that run from left to right, each corresponding to one of the teeth of the key. The lowest then will be numbered one. So this key can be read as three, one, two, one, four. Do you see?"

"How fascinating! But the key itself is of a particular shape."

"Yes, but all are based on a few distinct moulds. It is an art, and one of my many skills."

"Mrs Unsworth certainly chose the right man."

"And she chose the right mistress," he said. "For I know what you do for her family."

"Hush," she said, turning away and putting the key back in the drawer. "She does not."

"But—"

"Can you lock this drawer again?" she said.

"Certainly, Mrs C," he replied, and he bent to the task cheerfully.

As he wriggled the wire in the lock, she prowled around the rest of the study. It was furnished in a typical bachelor way and reminded her of Hugo Hawke's male domain. She wondered if they all bought their novelty globe drinks cabinets in the same shop which exclusively provided furnishings for bachelors' studies. She crossed to the fire and shook her head in disapproval when she saw that the grate had not been swept out.

On a small table by a comfortable-looking chair was a book, and she was curious to see what he was reading. It turned out to be The Count of Monte Cristo, but when she flipped it open, the bookmark was only a few pages in. He hadn't made much progress.

She was about to close it when she noticed that the bookmark was a note scribbled on a scrap of paper.

Coercion will fail. Look to your loyalties; speak not to me. B.

Her heart thudded. She grabbed it and thrust it into her pocket, and nearly squealed in surprise when something showered against the window.

Dodson ran past her and pressed against the glass, waving. "Mrs C, that is our signal to depart."

"Of course." She put the book down and hesitated. Wouldn't he notice that she had taken the note? She didn't understand it but she had a very strong suspicion as to its meaning.

"Mrs C!" Dodson said urgently.

Now her attention was caught by the fireplace once more. Socks had not been burning coal. She peered more closely. There was the ragged edge of fabric there, and white dust.

"Mrs C!" Dodson hissed. "I shall leave you here. Remember you must leave by the door unless you wish to strip yourself of your clothes..."

"Dash it!"

There was no more time to think. She followed him out of the room, down the stairs and through the main door. He remained within, and locked it, and within moments he had slithered out of the lower window.

Ruby was waiting for them in the street. She was frantic, and pointed to the right. "Geoffrey is there, arguing with the coach, and I assume it is Socks, so we must go."

They ran to the left, towards Stanley, and were joined by a breathless Geoffrey a few moments later.

"I hope your housebreaking was worth it," Geoffrey said. "I have been writhing around on the floor pretending to be quite mad. My jacket is ruined."

"I shall see that everyone is fully recompensed," she said. "Especially you, Dodson."

"I already have been, Mrs C," he said cheerfully, and opened his coat to reveal an array of small objects pilfered from the house of Albert Socks. "I already have been."

CHAPTER THIRTY-SIX

They all slept late the next morning, except for Neville Fry who was up and prowling about from dawn. The smell of silver polish seemed to hang in the air like a winter fog. Cordelia woke by slow degrees, coming to a gradual awareness as the recollections of the previous night's adventures ambled through her mind.

And then she was bolt upright in bed, and calling for Ruby.

"I know what we must do next!" she declared. "Come along. Get up and get yourself dressed. Help me get dressed. We must breakfast and go straight down to the police station house!"

"All at the same time?" Ruby grumbled. She shuffled off to the kitchen to seek out warm water.

***

Cordelia and Ruby walked together to Bow Street. Cordelia was brimming with excitement and determination. She carried a very precious parcel, well-padded, in her hands.

"This could be it, Ruby," she said as they neared the open doors of the station house. "We could soon have Florence Fry free at last, and the real murderer in irons!"

"We have much to do to effect that," Ruby said cautiously.

"Constable Evans!" Cordelia called and leaped forward. The young policeman was coming down the steps to the street and he looked wide-eyed at the apparition before him. Cordelia had insisted on dressing to the very highest standard. Nothing strikes fear into a man like a woman well-corseted with a high feathered hat, she had told Ruby, and her maid agreed.

Certainly, the look on Evans' face was bordering on terror.

"Good lady, my morning," he said. "Oh!"

She smiled at him, and wondered if the police would be a fitting career for her Stanley, who was similarly afflicted. "Good day," she said politely, as if he hadn't stumbled over his words. "I wonder if I might have a private talk with you. We need your help."

"I, oh, thank you. I have just finished my shift," he

said.

"Of course. We won't be long," she said, and she hustled him back up the steps into the stationhouse. "Any little office will do. Thank you."

He had no choice, trapped as he was in a pincer movement between Ruby and Cordelia. There was no sign of Inspector Hood and she was relieved about that.

Once they were in a small side room, she wasted no time. "Constable Evans, there is a girl in your cells who is not only entirely innocent of the crime she has been accused of, but in fact, she is a victim herself! A victim, being treated as a murderer. The situation is intolerable."

"Miss Fry, you mean, my lady?"

"The same. Now, she is the victim of a hateful campaign to push the blame onto her. This cannot be allowed to happen."

"But she goes to the Old Bailey next week, and there is no one else to stand trial for the deed," Constable Evans said. "I fear that she will be found guilty and she will hang, for sure."

"Absolutely not. Not while there are fine men like yourself who work tirelessly for justice."

He swallowed nervously. "But what can I do? I am just an ordinary man on the beat."

"Are we not all ordinary people yet called, sometimes,

to extraordinary things?" Cordelia did not glance at Ruby, who would be rolling her eyes by now. But the rhetoric was working on the constable. He was standing a little taller, and watching Cordelia with eyes of pride and hope, and not a little trepidation.

"Yes, my lady, perhaps…" he said.

"Marvellous. I knew that you would understand. Did I not say so, Ruby?" she said, without looking at her maid. "Now, we shall begin this important work, together. I am so glad you will help us. All we need is to see the evidence that has been gathered on Florence Fry. We shall wait here." She beamed at him expectantly.

He frowned, smiled, gaped, sighed, and licked his lips nervously. Once he had run through the gamut of emotions, he had nothing else left to do but to obey.

"I shall do what I can," he said, and disappeared.

He was not gone for long.

When he returned, he was carrying a large paste-board box, and he slid it onto the table. He nodded at the door and Ruby jumped to close it behind him. She stayed there, on guard against sudden unexpected intruders.

Cordelia put her own precious parcel on the table next to the box, and unwrapped the layers that protected it. "I believe a key was found in her possession," she said.

"Indeed," Constable Evans said, and dug in the box

until he pulled it free. "This is it."

She took it, and laid it onto the object she had revealed from the parcel's wrappings. "It matches!"

And it did. The key that Florence had used now lay in a perfect impression of its twin, nestling on a bed of hardened biscuit dough.

Cordelia clapped her hands. "The key that Albert Socks keeps is, indeed, the same as the one to her room. And, as we know, Ruby, all the rooms on that floor use this very key."

"That introduces some doubt, then, my lady," Ruby pointed out. "This key is not an exclusive pattern."

"It is enough, I think. I am sure of it," Cordelia said. "What else lies in this box?"

"See for yourself," he said, and stepped back.

She peered inside. There was the bottle of wine, now empty. She sniffed at the bottle but could detect nothing but a vinegar odour, and stale at that. There were Florence's gloves, and her small handbag. Inside that was a purse containing a few coins, a tortoiseshell comb, and a small pot that seemed to have cream within it. Separate to all that was a note.

Her heart leaped. *More clues*, she thought, and unfolded the paper to read what the message said.

It was thick and expensive paper, ragged at the edges,

with a definable laid pattern to it. The hand that had written the note was firm and steady, with looping letters, a pure and proper copperplate. "Where was the note found? In Florence's handbag?"

"I do not think so, my lady. It was in the room, yes. But it is from Miss Fry herself, I believe, to the deceased gentleman."

It was a simple and straightforward message. "Meet me at Mrs Clancey's tonight. Our usual room. F."

Ruby came from her post at the door to look at the letter. "Her handwriting's improved," she said.

Cordelia blinked. "Goodness, so it has." She still had the letter that Florence had sent to her father. She compared the two. Florence's original letter was childish and badly spelled.

This new note was perfect in every way.

"She did not write this note," Cordelia said. "This, then, is more evidence that this murder was arranged, and she was but a pawn in the affair!"

Before Constable Evans could protest, she put the key and the note in her own bag. She saw his look, and explained, "I cannot leave it to the police here; you understand that, don't you? I must take charge, now."

He nodded, a little unwillingly.

She took her leave before he could change his mind,

and try to stop her.

***

After such a good start to the day, Cordelia thought that things would continue to go well. Unfortunately, she spent the afternoon pacing the lodgings at Furnival's Inn, trying to work out how she was going to set up the final confrontation.

Ruby and Stanley were in the room, and Neville hovered by the open kitchen door, trying to work but failing to complete any task.

Cordelia sat, stood up, walked, sat, and generally huffed and puffed and sighed her way around the sitting room.

"We cannot leave this to the police," she said. "She will not go before the police court at Bow Street, so the fact that I know one of the magistrates there is of no help." She thought of Hugo Hawke, and his insistence that the police corruption that was thwarting him in Holborn was only to be solved by public exposure. Maybe he was correct.

"So," she continued, now standing at the window but not looking at anything in particular. "So ... I must confront Albert Socks in a public place, and in sight of persons of standing, and the law itself, and the general population. There must be witnesses so that his guilt is made unequivocally plain to all. I will demonstrate, with this actual evidence, that Florence did not write the note. I will demonstrate that Socks had a key to the room. I will explain how the murder was committed, and I also have the note from Socks' own house."

"I do not understand that note," Ruby said.

Cordelia read it out again. "Coercion will fail. Look to your loyalties; speak not to me. B."

"Brookfield?"

"Bonneville," Cordelia said. "It is clear that Socks has tried to coerce Bonneville because of his revolutionary politics. Socks wanted to change Bonneville's mind. Undeterred, Bonneville has continued, and sent this note to remind Socks that he cannot be coerced, and to leave him alone."

Ruby nodded. "I see."

"But where can I make this stand?" wailed Cordelia in frustration. "Must I go to Parliament myself and bang on the door like Black Rod until I am allowed in?"

"You could blow the doors off with gunpowder but a woman can never gain admittance," Ruby said.

Cordelia leaned her forehead against the cool glass of the window. "Come on, Stanley," she said. "You are the one who steps in at this moment and makes everything all right again."

"I am sorry, my lady, I am trying," he stammered.

"It's obvious."

314

Cordelia shot to the kitchen door. Geoffrey was sitting at the table, a scattering of food around him, and he was grinning. He nodded towards Stanley who had followed Cordelia.

"He knows, he does, the lad," Geoffrey went on. "You were talking about it last night and all."

"I know what?"

"You were mithering on about some lecture that you wished to attend but you felt you would not be welcome, on account of you just being some stable boy."

"I was," Stanley said. "Oh! My lady, perhaps it is the thing. For it is a political debate to be held, tonight, at some public rooms."

"What is the nature of the debate?"

"The famine in Ireland."

"Peel says there is no famine. He says it is an exaggeration."

"Not so," Stanley said, blushing at the arrogance of correcting his mistress. "The church I attend is very clear upon the matter. They are dying there, dying like dogs, falling to the ground by the side of the road, dying where they fall and where they lay."

Cordelia's flesh chilled and her goose bumps rose. "But can we be sure that Socks will be there?"

"We cannot."

"We can find out," said Ruby. "I will return to his house and speak to his staff once more. Stanley, if you please..."

He leaped to her side, and together they went out on their mission.

CHAPTER THIRTY-SEVEN

Many politicians had turned out for the lecture. Sir Robert Peel was losing his already-tenuous grip on his own party, never mind the whole country. Things looked bad for him. Many said that he knew that his days were now numbered, and that he was trying to push through as much legislation as he could before he had to resign — or, worse, another assassination attempt was made. The last one had led to the tragic death of his secretary.

Cordelia surrounded herself by her staff, and had made them all dress up as finely as they could. "You must look like the well-to-do liveried members of a good household," she had told them.

"You mean we're not?"

But they had responded, and now she approached the lecture hall, flanked by Ruby, Stanley and Geoffrey, all following a half-pace behind and fanning out like a train behind her.

It appeared to be a very popular lecture, or debate. Indeed, Cordelia was not quite sure what she was heading for. The topic of the night was a difficult one, and she was not sure which of the reports she'd heard were the right ones. And if there was a famine in Ireland, was it the role of the state to intervene? What had caused it? Foolish farming? Free trade? Many blamed the tendencies of the Irish poor themselves, as if they were animals not people; some of the things that Cordelia overheard made her sick and angry, though she recognised fear and misunderstanding in their words. She herself had never been to Ireland. Perhaps they were correct in what they said. Could people be so different, country to country?

She thought, then, she ought to travel even more widely, and see for herself.

"My lady!" Ruby's urgent hiss brought her back to herself. Ruby caught up and put up a hand to stop Cordelia. "Look, his footman was right in what he told me. There is Socks himself! I recognise the coach he is stepping down from. Look at that crest! Does he fancy himself as a lord, then?"

"Clearly he does," Cordelia said. "You are right. That is the ambitious little toad himself."

"Will you confront him here?"

"I don't know." Cordelia was buffeted on all sides now that she was closer to the entrance. She heard someone call her name, and saw Ivy and her husband who were approaching from the opposite direction. That put Socks right in the middle of them. "Yes," she said, decisively. "Now is the time!"

She stepped forward and raised her hand up high. "Albert Socks!" she said, trying to shout, but somehow a bout of nervousness had gripped her out of nowhere, and she merely squeaked.

She tried again. She needed to catch him before he entered the lecture hall. "Albert Socks! You are a murderer!"

That stopped him. In fact, it stopped everyone. He spun around and spotted her.

"Er ... good evening, my lady," he said, confusion all across his face. He didn't look remotely guilty or threatened. "Are you addressing me? Is this a parlour game gone wrong?"

"I am addressing you!" she declared and moved closer to him. "I am here to tell you that you are to be arrested for the murder of Florence Fry." There were policemen within earshot, and Mr Delaney the magistrate on hand too. How could she fail?

Easily.

Socks laughed. "Oh dear. London air and London

stress has had a terrible effect on you, my dear woman. Your maid must take you home directly."

"I have evidence," she said. She pulled out the key and the impression she had taken in dough.

"You have a biscuit," he said, and the nearest people laughed. She had already amassed a curious crowd.

"The key that was taken from Florence Fry is the same key that you had in your possession! You gained entry to the room that night."

He looked around at the expectant watchers, and smiled, playing to them. "Of course I have the same key. I rented that room and I have never denied it. She took a copy of the key, the foolish and duplicitous girl. She wanted to use that room for her own ends."

"But why did you rent such a room?" Cordelia said.

There was a low hum of laughter even before he answered, quite simply, "I am a man."

No, you're a fool, and that's quite different, she thought. She then brandished the note aloft. "They claim that this note was written by Florence, asking Bonneville to meet her there! But we have a letter from Florence and it clearly demonstrates that this note was a forgery."

"It only shows that one or the other might be a forgery, not which one," Socks said. He seemed to be enjoying himself. "Any other evidence, you poor dear?"

"This!" she said and held the final, coded message aloft. "From Bonneville himself, asking you to stop bullying him! You could never hope to coerce him to change his politics. So you killed him!"

His eyes widened when he recognised the note, and he took a step back. Mr Delaney had come up close beside him, and put out a steadying hand. The magistrate looked very serious, and very sad.

"My dear lady," he said, in a low voice. "I shall ask my Ivy to accompany you home, and I know a very good doctor who might be called upon at your earliest convenience."

"I am not ill, nor am I mad!" she said. "This is evidence!"

Mr Delaney shook his head. "It is with very great regret that I must inform you, my lady, that all your evidence is utterly useless."

"Why?" She fought to appear to be in control but it was hard as waves of anger made her hot. "Because the police are corrupt? Because he is a man of some influence? I do not believe it!"

"No," Mr Delaney said. "For Mr Socks was dining with me on the night that Louis Bonneville lost his life."

CHAPTER THIRTY-EIGHT

She stepped back. The crowd was roaring with laughter now, and her staff closed around her, fending off the pointing fingers and baying voices. Ivy, too, came up to her, and she looked distraught with worry.

"Dear Cordelia, come this way. You can use our carriage."

Cordelia could barely think straight. She stared as Albert Socks tipped his hat to her, very shallowly and rudely, and disappeared into the lecture hall. Mr Delaney waited at a respectful distance. Others mocked her as they passed. She heard a familiar voice and turned to see the tall, distinguished figure of Lord Brookfield. He was looking at her curiously.

She felt her face burn.

"You!" she said, suddenly, pointing at him. "It's you, it has been you all along, has it not?"

He shrugged. "My lady, you are unwell."

"It's you!" she said, her voice now rising in a shriek that took everyone by surprise. He had been at the party on the fateful night she had been abducted. Stanley had spoken to a well-dressed man. She had spoken too much of her suspicions, that night; he had become concerned and arranged for her kidnapping, surely!

He doffed his top hat completely, and came forward as if to perform a courteous bow. But when he was close enough to speak quietly, he simply said, "Well? Prove it."

Then he was swept away with the rest into the lecture hall, and the doors slammed, and she was left alone with her staff, and her long-faced friend Ivy.

***

Ivy Delaney was as good as her word. She hurried Cordelia into her carriage, and they began their journey back to Furnival's Inn. Ruby, Stanley and Geoffrey walked.

"I know that I am not the most popular person at parties and events," Ivy said to her as they made slow progress through the streets. "I know that I giggle and I talk a lot and I pry into much that is not my business. It was the same at school, if I am honest. The other girls seemed to band together and … oh! There I go, doing it again." She reached over and patted Cordelia's hand familiarly. "What I am trying to say is this: you can rely on me."

"And your husband?"

Ivy nodded, but she looked downcast. "It is true what he says."

"That he was dining with Socks?"

"Yes. And a few others."

Cordelia didn't know the magistrate well enough to believe him, but she knew Ivy now and she had the utmost faith in her. She sat back. "I have made a dreadful mistake."

"In accusing Mr Socks?"

"No. Yes. But no, mostly in showing my hand too soon. Now they all know what evidence I have."

"Yet the evidence, if I may be so bold, was wrong."

"No," said Cordelia, urgently. "No, the evidence still stands. It is simply my interpretation of the evidence which has been amiss. Ivy, may I call on you later?"

"Of course. I shall be at home all afternoon tomorrow. Please do. Ah, here we are, your lodgings."

Cordelia pressed Ivy's hand firmly. "Thank you. For everything."

***

Ruby and the others tumbled into the sitting room soon afterwards. Geoffrey had bought some meat pies, and

Stanley had bought some fine pastries. Ruby scurried through to make some tea, and Cordelia followed her. She drew the armchair up to the kitchen table and rested her elbows on the wooden top.

No one spoke for a while. Geoffrey stood, leaning on the wall, picking at his fingernails with a pocket knife. Stanley fidgeted, and Ruby busied herself with the kettle and teapot. There was no sign of Mrs Unsworth, nor of Neville Fry. It was evening, and she assumed they were both out.

When she looked up, she saw that all of them were looking at her, but no one was bold enough to be the first to speak. There was a tentative wariness in the air.

"Which of you thinks that I am mad, then?" she said at last.

"No, my lady!"

"Of course not."

Geoffrey coughed. "But a little misguided and hasty, perhaps."

"You didn't stop me."

"Could I have?"

He had a point.

"Do you really think it's Lord Brookfield now?" Ruby said.

"I am strongly suspicious of him. I have been, all along."

"No, you haven't."

Cordelia waved that away. "I have, underneath. Certainly I have been suspicious of some interactions between him and Albert Socks."

"But does the evidence point to Lord Brookfield?" Ruby asked. "The room was rented by Socks. The key was found in Socks' house. Even that note…"

"Ah, the note." Cordelia plucked it from her bag which was on the floor by her feet. She spread it on the table. "Coercion," she said. "That is not what I think it is."

"How can it be anything other?" Ruby said.

"This is a political matter," she said. "It's a term that I was not familiar with, but it is to do with a law or an act or something. This is to do with Bonneville, yes, but not in the way that I had thought."

"My lady," Stanley said, "may I say something?"

"Of course."

"You were kidnapped after that ball."

"Yes," she said, remembering how she had got drunk and brought shame on her name in front of … oh! In front of Lord Brookfield.

"And you accuse Lord Brookfield of being the murderer."

"I do."

"He is rich, he is powerful, and you have already found

your life in danger. By bringing this matter into the open so dramatically, do you not think that now, you are in double the amount of danger?"

"He can surely not act against me. Not again. It would be too obvious."

"He knows you have evidence, if you are correct in your assertion," Ruby said. "If you really think that your evidence will bring the killer to justice then you have just told him — potentially the killer — that you have the means for his downfall, right here, in your hands. You have given him even more reason to wish to do you harm."

"I am a threat," Cordelia said.

"You always have been."

Cordelia pulled the other note from her bag and put it on the table. "This handwriting is not from Florence, and nor does it match this message, which I am now convinced is from Lord Brookfield. So who sent the note asking Bonneville to meet Florence at Mrs Clancey's?" She stared at it.

"I suppose we are looking for someone who owns a red pen?" Ruby said.

"It is an unusual colour to — ah. There was something in Socks' desk also written in red. And look! There is a circle over the letter "i", too. Socks wrote this note. I am sure that if we obtained more written evidence from his possession that it would confirm what I am saying."

"So what's next, my lady?" Ruby asked. "Do we now pounce on Lord Brookfield with this evidence?"

"I suspect that things would go ill for me," Cordelia said. "However, something can be done. You told me to be clever, Ruby."

"I did."

"Then I shall. A clever person does not do something if they can ask another, with better skills, to do it for them."

"That is why you have servants, my lady."

"Indeed. And that is why a message must be conveyed to Hugo Hawke."

Her staff protested, but she wrote a note and ordered it to be conveyed to him that moment, irrespective of the late hour. "And you must wait for a reply."

"And if he is out?"

"Wait longer."

CHAPTER THIRTY-NINE

Mr Delaney was sceptical about her plan. "My dear Ivy has assured me that she has complete faith in you," he said, the next night, as they stood outside in the dark street with a light rain falling around them. "Yet I confess that I cannot fully understand why we must do it this way."

"He is guilty," she said. She was wrapped in her cloak with a hood pulled over her head, and wore sensible, unfussy clothing. Her "house-breaking" costume, as Ruby now referred to it. "I have the proof now, but the police in this division — your division, as you know — are not to be trusted. I am sure, now, that he is paying the detectives off."

"I have my own men," he said. "Faithful ones."

"And yet," she persisted, "what good has that done? You are a high-ranking man and perhaps that is an obstacle in some ways. Here, on the street, dreadful things are happening, all the time. And if I bring this evidence to the police, to Inspector Hood, right now, what do you think will happen? Brookfield has escaped justice and he will continue to do so. He will laugh at me. They will both laugh at me."

"And this way is better? I fail to see how forcing a confrontation will work. You have nothing new to say to him, have you?"

"I have," she said. "But far more important is the way that I say it. But there is one more thing. I am confident that I can extract a confession from him, in public."

"If you can, we will all be in your debt."

She smiled. "That is exactly what I hoped you would say. There is a favour you might do for me. Bow Street has the unusual capacity of having a kind of jurisdiction over the other Metropolitan divisions, am I right?"

"Indeed you are correct. We can step in anywhere, by virtue of our history as the headquarters of the old Runners."

"Excellent. For I have the help, tonight, of an … uh, acquaintance … who, in return, could do with some help in his own legal affairs north of here, in Holborn."

"If all goes to plan, then I shall do what I can."

"Thank you, sir," she said. "And here they come!"

"Good heavens," Mr Delaney said. "Have you raised an army?"

***

Hugo Hawke was at the head of the small band of very large men. "You are moon-struck," he said. "Quite, quite mad."

"And yet you have agreed to do this."

"I have."

She could not tell if he was smiling or grimacing. The faint light from the gas lamp overhead was reflected in his eyes, giving them a twinkle. But his voice was low and gruff. "Anyway," he said. "You asked, and I have delivered. Here they are. Eleven men, all in dark blue, with their coats and hats as close as I can make it so that they seem to be policemen. But you had better hope that it remains dark, and we that have no moon tonight, for the disguise will not hold to close inspection."

"The moon will be but a thin sliver, and I doubt we shall see it through the clouds," she said. "I am grateful indeed for the rain, and your presence."

"I am listed in the rank after rain? Charming," he said.

She could definitely hear a smile in the rogue's voice. She still had little respect for the man, but she was, truly, pleased that he was here, even if it was for his own purposes only.

"Come," he said. "We must go. Oh! Sir, I apologise..."

Mr Delaney came forward from the shadows into

which he had melted. There was a brief introduction, and then the genteel peace was interrupted by the arrival of Geoffrey who seemed to be carrying half of a blacksmith's shop with him.

"Just in case."

Cordelia nodded. "Thank you."

A look of startled horror passed between Hugo and the magistrate.

The assembled men were shuffling their feet, eager to be on their way.

"Hugo, can your men move swiftly and silently? I do not want to attract much attention in the streets."

He sighed. "Nearly half a dozen street-fighters and boxers, my lady, cannot blink without attracting attention. We had better get to this man's house, and start the business."

"Lead on," she said, but ignored her own remark and took to the front of the group.

***

Hugo strode to the left of her. Close behind them and trying to get in between them was Geoffrey. To her right was Mr Delaney. It was thrilling to have a posse of strong men following at her back.

334

"Which of these men could play the part of an arresting officer?" she said.

Mr Delaney cut in. "Do you not expect me to do that?"

"No, but I thank you, sir. He knows you, does he not?"

"He does."

"And I cannot do it," Hugo Hawke said. "Smith will do it. He can speak nicely enough, for a foundry-worker."

"Excellent," she said.

The magistrate then said, "I have one more concern. We cannot allow these men, rough as they are, to lay hands upon the Lord Brookfield. Even if you force a confession from him, which I am sceptical about, what then? Do you expect that he will come quietly with me?"

"No," she said. "Do not fear. I have other contacts hereabouts, and that is quite in hand."

Hugo said, "There is no point pressing her. She will have her way. I have learned this to my cost."

She ignored them both now. Lord Brookfield's house in London was a tall, narrow affair in Bloomsbury. The rain was keeping most people inside, though their little crowd had turned a few heads. There was not the same bustle on the streets in the more exclusive areas. Here, people could live fully inside. In the poor places, the dwellings were so cramped and dirty that family life existed as much outside as it did within the cracked and unsafe walls.

Gibbs had made enquiries for her, discreetly, and had discovered that to the best of his knowledge Lord Brookfield would be at home that midweek evening. She had not told him the full extent of her plans, because she knew he would worry.

And she, herself, was worrying. What if the information was wrong? Or what if he had changed his mind and gone out? She stared up at the house. There were lights in some of the windows, but that meant nothing.

Was he home?

Her chest felt tight.

He had to be home. She could not organise this lunacy, this folly, another time. If she stopped to think about what she was doing, she would have laughed, then cried, then committed herself to the nearest asylum.

What else could she do? Write to The Times? Take out an advertisement in The Daily Post? The only solution had to be a public confession, and she had to use all her skills of acting and artifice.

What is a woman, she thought, *if not someone who has had to learn to survive in this world by her acting, and artifice, and conversational cunning? This is truly what all my education has led me to. This is what we are all bred to, in the end.*

She pushed away her doubts. "Hugo, bring me your man, Smith."

A very tall man with wide shoulders but a narrow waist was brought to her. He dipped his head in respect briefly, but then met her eyes as she talked to him. He reminded her of Geoffrey, a man secure enough in his place to fear no one of any standing, higher or lower.

She explained, at length, what he was to say. "Can you remember all this?" she demanded.

"Of course," he replied, and he spoke with confidence. "Go to it, then."

He rolled his shoulders as if adjusting his jacket, and then strode up the steps to the door. She hastily placed the other fake policemen all around, and hid herself with Hugo, Mr Delaney, and Geoffrey at the back.

Smith hammered loudly. The door was answered very promptly by a liveried man.

"Can I help you?" the overdressed flunky inquired.

"We are here on the business of justice," Smith said, his voice strong. "We are to arrest the Lord Brookfield and take him into custody."

The man in livery laughed. "You are not serious. Get off this property."

Smith pushed forward, and Cordelia cheered inside. He wedged himself in the doorway and shouted, "Lord Brookfield! You must show yourself or we shall come in and take you by force."

"You cannot! This is a disgrace!" The manservant shoved at Smith, who shoved back.

"Assault a member of the police, would you? Arrest this man, too!"

Lord Brookfield then appeared behind them, in the hallway, lit by the lamps and candles that adorned his large home. He was dressed for a quiet evening alone, in a rich smoking jacket and comfortable trousers. "What is going on here?" he demanded.

"Lord Brookfield? You are arrested for the murder of Louis Bonneville. You must come with us, sir." Smith then waved his arms to get two more men to join him on the steps. Cordelia was impressed.

Lord Brookfield laughed, just as his manservant had done a moment before. "Oh, get them away from here, Travers."

"We have evidence, sir."

"Oh, you haven't been listening to that poor, ill Lady Cordelia have you? She's not right in the head. She is a widow, you know."

As if that explains anything, she thought crossly. Although it was an excuse she had often used to justify her erratic behaviour, it was not one that she wished to have foisted on herself.

"We have a confession from Albert Socks, sir. He has

confessed to his part in the crime, and to your own most fatal involvement."

"You have a *what?* From Socks?"

"Indeed, sir. He is at the station house at this very moment, telling us all."

"That two-faced, lying, duplicitous little —! Why, I warned him ..."

Mr Delaney, at Cordelia's side, hissed in surprise.

"So you see, sir," Smith was continuing. "We have evidence and a confession. It is inevitable."

"Look, man," Lord Brookfield said, suddenly lowering his voice. "This is all so loud and unnecessary. You have a man in custody now, so go along with Albert Socks. Goodness knows, he will be no great loss to the political community. Travers, some money, if you will."

"I cannot take a bribe," Smith said proudly.

Now Mr Delaney was positively fuming.

"It is not a bribe," Lord Brookfield said. He lowered his voice even further so that they could no longer hear what was being said but he gesticulated inside and was clearly inviting Smith to step in and discuss terms.

Smith stepped back, and motioned his men forward, and said in a clear voice, "I will not! Men, arrest him. You will be charged with perverting the course of justice, with the attempted corruption of an officer of the law, and murder!"

"Your Smith is really very good. Maybe he should consider a career in the police himself," Cordelia whispered to Hugo.

"And take a pay cut, for terrible hours, and the daily threat of violence? He is better working at an honest job," Hugo replied.

"I am innocent!" Lord Brookfield was saying. "This is just slander and lies. You cannot believe anything that Socks says."

Smith pulled out the trump card that Cordelia had furnished him with. It was the coded message that she had found in Albert Socks' study. "And this, sir? This note that you wrote, on your own notepaper, with the heading torn off, to Socks? It condemns you, sir."

"It is not mine and I have never seen it before. Get off my property!"

"When you hold it to the light, sir, your watermark, your family crest, is fully visible."

Lord Brookfield lunged forward but he was immediately grabbed by two of the boxers and the rest rushed up the steps to surround him and bring him down, jostling and pushing.

Cordelia stepped forward. She had no one left to hide behind now, and she brought herself out into the light.

"You!" he yelled in fury. "I might have guessed!"

Now her other confederates were arriving and moving towards them, watching and listening.

"Yes, me," she said. "You are condemned by your own mouth, and by your hand, and by your deeds, now that I have unravelled it all."

"Why?"

"Because you are guilty."

"No, why would I want to kill a member of my own party?"

"You were hardly on the same side," she said. "You have made that very plain to me. You are a man of tradition, of history, of stability. You do not even like what your own party leader is doing! I understand what 'coercion' means now. It refers to the Bill that Peel wants to bring before Parliament, the Irish Coercion Bill, and you oppose it. You oppose all that he stands for. You oppose free trade and progress and the repeal of the corn laws."

"I oppose a man who has turned from a Tory to a Whig! He is a liberal in disguise, my lady, and you know nothing of what you speak!"

"And Bonneville was more radical even than Peel," she said. "Peel still has his supporters in the house, but when Bonneville was killed, he had one less, and it sent a signal to the rest. Constable Evans?" she called.

"I am here, my lady."

"Arrest this man."

Smith and the boxers fell away as the real policemen came up and took hold of Lord Brookfield.

"What is this? Was this a sham? A trick? This is—"

He was hauled away, and suddenly Cordelia was surrounded by a throng of laughing and celebratory fighting men, all slapping one another's backs.

"That was good sport," said Smith. "Now, let us take you to show you our kind of sport..."

CHAPTER FORTY

Even Hugo was alarmed at the suggestion that Cordelia attend a boxing match. She was urged into a cab instead, and Mr Delaney accompanied her. "We must go to the station house now, and set things right," he explained. "Your Mr Hawke, and your coachman, and that Smith must come also. Constable Evans and his men will take the Lord Brookfield."

"Do you think he can really face justice?" she asked as they rattled through the drizzling streets. Her cloak had kept her dry, but her feet were wet and the moisture had wicked up her fine woollen stockings steadily.

"I hope so. This is the New Police, don't forget. We have had some issues but the principles remain sound. And the good men do outnumber the bad."

When they reached the station house, they discovered that word had preceded them, and the place was abuzz.

Albert Socks had been brought in and the two detectives that had been so rude to her were now claiming everything as their own.

She was taken into a small room, and insisted that Mr Delaney come too, so that her words could not be twisted, and she told them everything. Smith had handed over the message and they confirmed that it looked likely to be from Brookfield, not Bonneville.

Then she was asked to wait while they went about their enquiries, following her information and her hints. She was put in a small room, but this time it was not locked.

Ruby came from Furnival's Inn, and Geoffrey left briefly to obtain some food for them. Cordelia picked at it. "Oysters at last," she said. "Thank you."

"It was all I could obtain," he said. "I'm sorry."

"Don't be. It has been an extraordinary night."

"But this is not extraordinary food."

"Exactly," she said. "It will ground me."

Ruby laughed. "I think it would take more than rough street food to ground you, my lady! What do we wait here for?"

"News. I could go home but I need to know the outcome of all this. And anyway, the police might need my help again."

"I think they would rather eat a bad oyster," Ruby said.

"Your name is not spoken of with great praise out there."

"Only because they seek to take the credit for themselves, and they cannot."

But they could.

Constable Evans came to her at nearly midnight, when her eyelids were dropping. Ruby had fallen asleep in a chair, and Geoffrey was sitting on the floor. "Your butler is here," Evans said. "Come to take his daughter. I thought you might like to see her."

"Thank you! Yes, I will." She followed him to the lobby where Florence stood at the desk. Another policeman was writing things down in a ledger, while Neville Fry stood at his daughter's side, flapping his hands awkwardly.

"My darling child!" he said.

She looked at him as if he were a stranger — which, indeed, he was. "What is to become of me now?"

"We can find you a suitable position." He looked to Cordelia, who nodded.

"Of course. I have many kindly contacts." Well, she knew Ivy Delaney. That would be a start.

"I do not want to be in service!" Florence said haughtily. "I was engaged to be married to a powerful man, you know. I do not want a future as a maid."

"But you were used," Cordelia said. "Can you not see that, now?"

"We were in love," Florence insisted. "They said, that Inspector and his men, they said that Bonneville had been set up to fall for me, but I cannot believe it."

Neville tried to take her arm but she shook him off. She flounced out of the station house and he followed, dejectedly. Cordelia shook her head in sorrow, and noticed that Inspector Hood was watching her.

"Tell me about the relationship between her and Bonneville," she said. "What have you discovered?"

He smiled smugly. "Oh, I thought you knew everything," he said.

"You know that I do not."

He was triumphant, and in a most unseemly fashion. "We have decided to drop the charges of house-breaking against you, although the manner in which you obtained the evidence was very suspect. If one of my own men had acted in such a fashion, I would have had to have sacked him."

"Lucky, then, that it was me not them."

"Indeed. We have returned to Mrs Clancey's and have confirmed that the panel in the wardrobe was false, and that Socks not only rented one room, but both; he had the adjoining one, too, and the key fitted both doors."

"I knew it!"

"And on the night of the murder, he arranged for

Florence to be there, and for the Lord Brookfield himself to be in the adjoining room."

"He arranged?"

"Well, at the Lord Brookfield's insistence that he arrange things, so that Lord Brookfield himself could add the poison to the wine. Both of them knew that Florence would not drink it, and would be a perfect person to blame."

"And what of Socks and Brookfield?"

"Complicated," Hood said. "Once they were friends, and Brookfield his mentor, but lately they are more and more estranged. Both are odious in their own ways."

"And there, sir, we can agree," she said.

He twitched and hesitated before saying, "Yes, I believe we can. Now, my men are working on the investigations and we are satisfied that this will go to trial very soon."

She waited for his thanks, but none were forthcoming and she realised they never would be.

"Good evening, Inspector Hood," she said. "Let me fetch my maid and coachman, and I will be away."

"Do not leave London yet," he said. "We may yet ..."

"Need me?"

"...have to talk to you," he concluded.

***

347

Mrs Unsworth was remarkably sober for the late hour. She had been waiting in the kitchen, and even seemed relieved to see them all arrive back safely. She made some hot drinks without being asked.

Geoffrey was feeling very pleased with himself. He sat at the table and stretched. "They have even sacked some of the worst policemen," he said.

"I am still surprised that some of them are corrupt," Cordelia said. "And saddened."

Geoffrey shrugged. "What do you expect, when we take such rough men and put them on rough beats, and expect them to act like gentlemen?"

"Why, you almost sound as if you are sympathetic."

He snorted, and reached out for a biscuit. Before Cordelia could stop him, he had bitten deep into the dough that had an impression of the key on it.

"Geoffrey! Don't eat the evidence!"

CHAPTER FORTY-ONE

Cordelia woke unexpectedly early the next morning. She felt groggy and yet restless and she knew she would not be able to return to sleep. She crept out of bed, and left Ruby undisturbed.

She thought that she would find the kitchen empty, but Mrs Unsworth was already up. "My lady," she said. "One moment and the water will be hot enough for some tea."

"Thank you."

"Go through; I will bring it along directly."

"It is chilly in the sitting room. Allow me to sit by the range, if you will."

Mrs Unsworth nodded slightly, and set about her business.

Something had changed in her cook.

Cordelia wondered if Dodson had spoken with her, or

something else had happened.

"Mrs Unsworth, about your son, Jasper..."

Mrs Unsworth was facing away from Cordelia, and her back went rigid. "It's perfectly all right, my lady."

"You blame me for his incarceration, don't you?"

She did not reply.

Cordelia said, "I did all I could to have his sentence commuted. You are lucky that he has lived."

"Lucky? Is that a life, there, in that place?" She slammed the kettle back onto the top of the range, and gripped the metal rail, wrapping her fingers around the cloths that were hung there to dry. "But then, I have visited him, twice now, since we came here to London. And he tells me that I should thank you, after all."

"I am sorry that I could not have done more."

"So I am," she replied with her usual note of bitterness. "Actually, my lady, if we are to deal in honesty today, I thought that he would have been better to have hanged for what he did. Instead you thought you were doing him a favour by prolonging his life. I did not."

"Oh."

"But he does not see it that way that I saw it, and I did not know until lately. Here, your tea. Do you want breakfast?"

The conversation was clearly over, and it was more

than Cordelia had ever expected. "Some eggs, lightly done. Thank you."

***

Septimus Gibbs was supposed to escort her to the Old Bailey so that she could witness the trial, but he was called away at the last minute, and sent his profuse apologies.

She sent a note to Ivy and her husband, but no reply came back. She paced the room and in desperation, Ruby went out and returned half an hour later with the last person she wanted to see.

"Mr Hawke."

"Ha! When you want something from me, it's Hugo. Now I am no longer needed, it's back to Mr Hawke, is it? Yet you need me today. I understand a chaperone is required."

"I am awaiting a reply from Ivy Delaney and Mr Delaney."

"You'll not get one in time. Come on. We can walk there and I can tell you all my news."

"I have no interest in your news."

"You should have," he said, offering his arm, which she flatly refused to take. "It concerns you, in a way."

She flared her nostrils but she called Ruby. "Do wait while I change for walking out," she said.

They walked briskly. "Most of the trials there last but nine or ten minutes," Hugo told her. "They bring them in and send them out, almost on a rotation."

"I should imagine the Lord Brookfield's trial will be somewhat longer," she said.

"Why? He is guilty, and there is little to be said about it."

"I hope they might call me as a witness," she said.

He laughed. "As a scourge, perhaps."

"You should be grateful to me."

His tone did soften. "And I am grateful, but I shall only say this once, and then we shall never speak of it again."

"He did arrange to have me kidnapped, you know," she told him. "It was lucky for him that Stanley's carriage was stolen as it gave him more time to conjure things. He claims he had nothing to do with the mugging of Stanley and Ruby, though. No one cares about that."

"Why would they? It happens every hour, every day," Hugo said. He looked at her sideways and caught her expression. "I am sorry. I do not mean to sound as if I think that's acceptable. But it is the way of things."

"I know. Now, regarding your matter. I assume you spoke with Mr Delaney? Is everything arranged to your satisfaction?"

"I think that everything is arranged as well as it could be," he said. "It is not perfect, but your pet magistrate did indeed step in, and insist in some changes in the Holborn division. And no common magistrate he, but a real serjeant-at-law, you know."

"I knew."

"And it is well that he is so high. They have weeded out some of the less honest policemen there, and they have assured me my publican and my licence is quite safe. I must take care to remain within the boundaries of the law, at least outwardly."

"And inwardly!"

"You know me, Cordelia," he said with a grin. "Outward appearance is one thing; what lies beneath is quite another."

"You make yourself sound as if you have greater depths than you really do," she said.

"Hark at you! Ah, here we are. Do take my arm, Cordelia. For the look of the thing."

"For outward appearances, then," she said, and complied, but gripped it a little too tightly, for he deserved a bruise to remember her by.

***

He escorted her home again, and left her as soon as he could, for she was in a bad mood when she flounced back into Furnival's Inn. Ivy was waiting, having received the note, and was taking tea in the sitting room. Ruby was flitting about, helping the rest of the staff to pack up for their return to Clarfields.

"My dear!" cried Ivy, getting to her feet and rushing to Cordelia. "What ails you? Was the courtroom quite dreadful? Oh — no, tell me that he was not acquitted!"

"He was not, at least," Cordelia said, sulkily stripping off her gloves and letting them drop to the table. Ruby snatched them up with a sigh and took them to mend and clean.

"Then what happened?"

"It was very fast and very dull," she said. "I could barely see, on account of the press of men, all from newspapers and magazines, standing up and shouting. The judge was most blasé. He told the Lord Brookfield he was guilty, ordered the jury to find him so, and was reaching for his black cap before the foreman and the jury had barely returned. I did not think that it would happen so!"

"It is a busy court," Ivy said, taking her seat again. "But I do not understand why you can be so upset if he was found guilty! What of Socks?"

"Oh, guilty also. They are both to hang for it. No, the

problem is, my dear Ivy, that I sat there and no one mentioned me! No one asked for my statements or my deductions. No one knew of me and my work at all!"

"And did you do this for fame?"

"No, of course not. I did it for my butler, Mr Fry. And I did it for justice, which is a fine thing."

"Indeed it is," said Ivy.

"But it would be nice to have a little recognition! I have lost my column and I really do not know what I ought to do next."

"Go travelling," Ivy said, and it reminded Cordelia of some of her earlier ruminations on the narrowness of her experiences.

"Perhaps I should," she said. "I do have a fancy to see another country."

"Japan!" said Ruby with excitement. "Or France! Or the Americas, what of them?"

"Well, I was actually thinking of Wales..."

***

"This will cheer you up."

Cordelia had almost fallen asleep, in spite of the noise of the travelling chariot's wheels on the rough road from the railway station to Clarfields. Neville Fry had gone on ahead with Stanley and Mrs Unsworth. Geoffrey drove the chariot and nestled within were only Cordelia and Ruby.

"What will?" Cordelia said, blinking awake.

Ruby passed her the newspaper, folded back on itself for ease of handling.

"See there," Ruby said. "The gossip column next to the advertisement for hygienic woollen undergarments."

"How practical. Oh, yes, I have it." Cordelia read the coded sentences, and then began to laugh. "Ah! Recognition at last, then?"

"Indeed so. I thought you would be pleased."

One Brook brooks no opposition from another Brook. The lady prevails; and the lord hangs for it.

She re-read it. Just two sentences, and it meant that she was likely to be the talk of every salon and meeting and gathering in the city.

She pulled the curtain aside and peered out of the window. "We have some distance to go yet," she complained. "I do hope the railways come closer to Clarfields."

"I fully expect to wake up with a steam engine on the front lawn, the rate at which they are laying new track," Ruby said.

Cordelia let the curtain fall and read the rest of the gossip column. Much of it was incomprehensible, or open to interpretation. She decided she would write to Ivy and stay in touch with London's rumours and doings. She would return, she vowed. She'd finally begun to remake connections since her husband's death, and these new friendships were on her own terms. It was exciting.

She flicked through the rest of the paper. Sir Robert Peel was still on shaky ground and many now were calling for his resignation. A policeman had been attacked and was sorely injured. A scandalous new play had opened, run two nights, and been closed down for immorality. There was more and more of that, these days. It was as if society was lacing itself up ever more tightly.

She gave the paper back to Ruby and stretched her legs out. Her feet kicked a box that was under the opposite seat. She couldn't remember what was in it; most of the luggage was strapped to the top and back of the carriage. She leaned forward and pulled it out.

"Oh, yes," Ruby said. "I forgot to tell you but Geoffrey went out on a bit of a mission before we left London."

Cordelia opened the box and began to laugh. Stacked within was every kind of street food. Some, she saw, would not survive the journey much longer. There were jars of pickled periwinkles, and a sheep's trotter wrapped in paper. There was a collection of unmarked pies, which she set aside for later dissection rather than consumption. There was a brace of saveloy, the cold sausages tied up together like they were to be hung in a game cellar. There was a pale box of thin wicker which contained a selection of cheeses which smelled worse than the dried fish which nestled next to the box.

"Do you know, they eat seaweed in Wales?" Cordelia said, pulling some bread free and sitting back to scatter crumbs like a child.

"Why? Have they nothing else?"

"It is a delicacy. I must try it."

"You are set upon it, then?" Ruby asked.

"Of course."

"What part? Some areas, I am told, are wild and they speak a strange language there."

"I don't know yet," Cordelia said, "but I am sure there will be something useful I can do while I am there…"

"You're hoping for a murder, aren't you?"

Cordelia affected shock and disgust. "Ruby! I am ashamed of you. I would hope for no such thing."

Cordelia turned her head away and hid her smile.

With a full belly, and a sense of satisfaction, she fell asleep again as she journeyed back to her home.

HISTORICAL NOTE

Inns of Court – Furnival's Inn was as described in the text and Dickens rented rooms here from December 1834 until 1837. That building was demolished in 1878.

Harriet Martineau existed; she was a well-known political writer of the day.

Sir Robert Peel is a man of some local repute here in Lancashire. It is impossible to summarise his politics and policies in this note, but the hints in the book should be a start if you are interested. He probably knew his days in office were numbered and indeed he resigned in June 1846, not long after the setting of this story. He founded the modern police force, and repealed the hated Corn Laws. He is also noted for downplaying the terrible tragedy that was unfolding in Ireland.

Eating in London — I regret to say that I have taken liberties. The place that Cordelia and Socks meet, which I have called a dining room or eating house, is a bit of a far-fetched idea, if I'm honest. Women of a higher status had very little choice about where they ate. They would dine at home, and that was it. The lower classes, and men, had a wider choice, with cookshops and bakeshops and street vendors, coffee shops, taverns, chophouses, oyster rooms, and inns. Restaurants, as we know them, were not known of until the 1860s in England.

The best resource for Victorian London is a book by Judith Flanders called The Victorian City.

Do email me if you have any corrections, concerns or queries – issy@issybrooke.com – or start a conversation on my facebook page.

Made in the USA
San Bernardino, CA
10 December 2016